W9-CJX-668

Congratulations to Arthur,
1923.

Clara. A. Case.

THE GIANT FLYING BOAT HEADED IN BETWEEN THE TALL
PINNACLES OF ICE.

Tom Swift and His Flying Boat.   *Page* 162

TOM SWIFT AND HIS FLYING BOAT

OR

The Castaways of the Giant Iceberg

By

VICTOR APPLETON

AUTHOR OF "TOM SWIFT AND HIS MOTOR CYCLE,"
"TOM SWIFT IN CAPTIVITY," "TOM SWIFT AND
HIS ELECTRIC LOCOMOTIVE," "THE MOVING
PICTURE BOYS SERIES," ETC.

ILLUSTRATED

NEW YORK
GROSSET & DUNLAP
PUBLISHERS

Made in the United States of America

BOOKS FOR BOYS
By VICTOR APPLETON

12mo.   Cloth.   Illustrated.

THE TOM SWIFT SERIES

TOM SWIFT AND HIS MOTOR CYCLE
TOM SWIFT AND HIS MOTOR BOAT
TOM SWIFT AND HIS AIRSHIP
TOM SWIFT AND HIS SUBMARINE BOAT
TOM SWIFT AND HIS ELECTRIC RUNABOUT
TOM SWIFT AND HIS WIRELESS MESSAGE
TOM SWIFT AMONG THE DIAMOND MAKERS
TOM SWIFT IN THE CAVES OF ICE
TOM SWIFT AND HIS SKY RACER
TOM SWIFT AND HIS ELECTRIC RIFLE
TOM SWIFT IN THE CITY OF GOLD
TOM SWIFT AND HIS AIR GLIDER
TOM SWIFT IN CAPTIVITY
TOM SWIFT AND HIS WIZARD CAMERA
TOM SWIFT AND HIS GREAT SEARCHLIGHT
TOM SWIFT AND HIS GIANT CANNON
TOM SWIFT AND HIS PHOTO TELEPHONE
TOM SWIFT AND HIS AERIAL WARSHIP
TOM SWIFT AND HIS BIG TUNNEL
TOM SWIFT IN THE LAND OF WONDERS
TOM SWIFT AND HIS WAR TANK
TOM SWIFT AND HIS AIR SCOUT
TOM SWIFT AND HIS UNDERSEA SEARCH
TOM SWIFT AMONG THE FIRE FIGHTERS
TOM SWIFT AND HIS ELECTRIC LOCOMOTIVE
TOM SWIFT AND HIS FLYING BOAT

THE MOVING PICTURE BOYS SERIES

THE MOVING PICTURE BOYS
THE MOVING PICTURE BOYS IN THE WEST
THE MOVING PICTURE BOYS ON THE COAST
THE MOVING PICTURE BOYS IN THE JUNGLE
THE MOVING PICTURE BOYS IN EARTHQUAKE
    LAND
THE MOVING PICTURE BOYS AND THE FLOOD
THE MOVING PICTURE BOYS AT PANAMA
THE MOVING PICTURE BOYS UNDER THE SEA
THE MOVING PICTURE BOYS ON THE WAR FRONT
THE MOVING PICTURE BOYS ON FRENCH
    BATTLEFIELDS
THE MOVING PICTURE BOYS' FIRST SHOW HOUSE
THE MOVING PICTURE BOYS AT SEASIDE PARK
THE MOVING PICTURE BOYS ON BROADWAY

GROSSET & DUNLAP, Publishers, New York

COPYRIGHT, 1923, BY
GROSSET & DUNLAP

Tom Swift and His Flying Boat

CONTENTS

iii

TOM SWIFT AND HIS FLYING BOAT

CHAPTER I

AN IDEA AND A FORTUNE

"I AM sure we can build such a flying boat, father."

"Humph! I wish I had your confidence, Tom," chuckled Mr. Barton Swift, the old inventor.

His son laughed, too. "It isn't confidence you lack," he said. "It is just that you are too cautious to seem optimistic."

"Have it your own way," rejoined his father. "Just the same, a speed boat for the air, land, and sea that will do all you suggest is something to consider fearfully. Nothing to compare to it has ever yet been launched."

"But it will be launched," cried Tom Swift eagerly. "Somebody will put it into the air before we know it. Why not get ahead of the rest of the smart folks? Why not put out a flying boat that will make all their eyes bug out?"

"Even your slang gets ahead of me, Tom," said his father mildly. "Just why do you wish to strain the optic nerves of your competitors?"

But Tom Swift only laughed. He knew just how young his father's mind remained, even if he was a semi-invalid at times and his body was weakened by age and hard work.

"There is a bunch of rich men, I understand, who mean to build a flying boat to go hunting in up toward the Arctic Circle next summer. There are others that believe the mystery of the Antarctic can only be revealed through the use of such a craft. The interior of Africa, around Lake Tanganyika and the other great lakes can be properly explored only by the use of some such machine. Central South America can be reached more easily from the Amazon and its great branches than by any other means. Without a flying boat, how may one fly over the falls and escape the dangers of the rapids?"

"Good! Good!" exclaimed Mr. Barton Swift. "I see you have been thinking this thing out, at least. A great many people have excuses for what they want to do; but you, Tom, have a reason. What else?"

Tom Swift laughed again. He was a boyish fellow, in spite of all his experiences of the past few years; and a boy finds it difficult at most times to take older people into his confidence, especially about his dreams and hopes.

"I do not know that my suggestion should seem an impossibility," Tom said, soberly. "See what the Swift Construction Company has done in the past. Of course, I am counting on your help, father, to carry such a thing to a successful conclusion."

"You actually talk as though you had conceived a plan and would put it into effect, Tom!" cried his father.

"I don't know but I have—and will," said Tom, smiling once more. "At any rate, I have been revolving the scheme in my head for a long time. I admit it. A flying boat, as the story-book fellows write now, has 'intrigued' my interest. I'm coocoo about it, to use Ned Newton's slang."

"So you lay your knowledge of the argot to Ned?" laughed Mr. Swift. "But this flying boat?"

"A lot has been accomplished by other people. We would not be the first in the field, by any means. But I believe I have some ideas about such an invention that would put us ahead of everybody else. And that is the main thing."

"The main thing, I should say, would be to have a working hypothesis of the idea in question," observed Barton Swift dryly. "What would you build a flying boat for? To what particular use is it to be put? Therefore, in making plans for the boat, they must fit the needs of the craft as devised.

"In other words, Tom, what in the world do you want a flying boat for? You have your air scout, your aerial warship that you sold to the Government during the war, your air glider which as yet has not been equaled, your sky racer, and your old *Red Cloud* which scarcely any newer airship marvel has surpassed. You have been up in the air enough, it seems to me. Why not tackle the practical inventions of peace, as I pointed out in your last marvel, the electric locomotive?"

"Give me an idea," grumbled Tom. "What shall I build—a new plough? Huh!"

"Say, Mist' Tom! tells yo' what," burst into the controversy an altogether unexpected voice.

The Swifts had been talking on the side piazza of their house near the works of the Swift Construction Company at Shopton. Just inside one of the rear windows a grizzled old colored man was busy preparing vegetables for dinner.

"I tells yo' what!" repeated Eradicate Sampson, the old serving man who had been with the Swifts for years and considered himself quite one of the family. "I tells yo' what! Yo' want to invent somethin' practical like yo' fader says, yo' make a machine that'll scoop the eyes out o' 'taters widout wastin' none o' de meat. Dat wot yo' do. Den yo' sho' nuff do somethin' wuth while."

Mr. Barton Swift burst into a laugh, as he almost always did when Eradicate Sampson, or "Rad" for short, made one of his suggestions. Even Tom, earnest as he was about the flying boat, grinned.

"I'll take that up some day and fix it for you, Rad," the young fellow said.

"Hope yo' does it 'fore I done git all dis bag of 'taters used up. Dey is sho' right eye-y. Sho' is!"

"If you want to carp and criticize at 'English as she is spoke,' there's your chance, father," grumbled Tom. "Look after Rad. But this flying boat idea—a craft that will sail on the water, roll on the ground, and fly through the air——"

"Old stuff, Tom," Mr. Swift answered bruskly. "There are very good inventions of that nature already."

"Quite true," admitted Tom, but not at all discouraged. "But none of them so far built would satisfy me if I were the inventor and builder."

"Ah-ha!"

"There are faults in every one already launched. I bet there are faults in all those now under construction, no matter how much money there may be behind the invention. I am going after the perfect flying boat, or I'll not build any."

"Well? Tell me how you will overcome the rough-sea obstacle, for instance?" asked the very practical Mr. Swift. "That has been puzzling the flying boat folks ever since the beginning. It is unsafe to descend in a heavy sea, therefore they dare not take long voyages from land."

"I mean to overcome that very thing if I tackle the thing at all."

"You speak very confidently, my son," said his father, looking at Tom seriously.

"I have thought about the invention for some time."

Mr. Barton Swift threw up his hands in mock despair.

"Incurable!" he cried. "Once you get your teeth set in a thing, Tom, there is no shaking you loose."

"I come honestly enough by that trait of character," said Tom, with a grin. "They say I'm a chip off the old block."

He sat up suddenly in his reclining chair and stared toward the front of the house. Idly at first he had heard the noise of a motor-car arriving before the house. It had stopped there. Mr. Swift had not appeared to notice it at all, but Tom suddenly overheard voices.

"Yes, sah. Dey is at home, but dey mebbe is

engaged on 'portant business," said a sonorous voice that could belong to nobody save Koku, Tom's giant servant whom the young inventor had brought with him some years before from far parts, and who had served him well and faithfully ever since.

"I isn't sure, sah. But I go see," went on the important sounding Koku.

"Listen to dat giant!" grumbled old Rad Sampson. "Jes' to hear him, yo'd think he was bossin' dis hyer fambly. Sho' nuff! Huh!"

The ancient colored man and the half-civilized Koku were sworn enemies up to a certain point. Both professed to scorn the other's efficiency and abilities. And both usurped the authority of speaking for either Tom or his father on almost any occasion.

But now Koku had tried the patience of the visitor. Overtopping the giant's serious tones came the sharper and more excited voice that Tom immediately recognized. And what the voice said startled even the placid Mr. Swift.

"Tom Swift! Tom Swift!" exclaimed the visitor. "Bless my telescope, Tom Swift, but I must see you! I must see you at once! Tom Swift!"

"Ho!" cried Tom, starting up. "Ho, Koku! Bring Mr. Damon right out here."

Hearing the young inventor's voice, Mr. Wakefield Damon waited for nothing more. He rushed around the corner of the house, appearing in an excited and a rather disheveled state upon the side porch where the two Swifts were sitting.

"Bless my decrepit extremities!" exclaimed the emphatic gentleman, thus referring to his own feet as they stumbled over a low ottoman and a rumpled mat. "I'm so excited I can't even walk straight. It's the greatest—well, how-do, Barton Swift? And you, Tom—how are you?"

Both his hosts welcomed the eccentric Wakefield Damon warmly. He was a good friend.

"What good wind has brought you here, Damon?" asked Mr. Swift, giving the visitor his hand.

"No such element as wind," declared Mr. Damon, with his usual energy. "Air, fire and water—the three principal elements. Nothing like air. It's frozen water has brought me here, I reckon," and he burst into a great laugh at his own fantasy. "Ice has brought me here, not wind."

"I heard your motor-car," said Tom smiling. "You don't mean to say you have invented a way of running a car with ice for fuel?"

"Nothing like that! Nothing like that!" cried Mr. Damon. "The gasoline people still rob me. But listen! I've got ice in my head—and some brains, I hope," he added. "At any rate, I know where to come for help when I get stuck in anything."

"You bring us a problem, do you?" asked Mr. Swift. "Well, Damon, what is it?"

"I have got to have Tom's help. I want him to take a journey with me."

"A journey—just now—when I've so much on my hands?" demanded the young inventor, in considerable doubt.

"I'll make it worth your while," said Mr. Damon quickly. "I've got to go to Iceland. There's money in it——"

"Money in Iceland?" interrupted Tom.

"So they tell me. And a lot of it is mine," returned the excited visitor. "I want you to go there with me, Tom, to get a fortune. A fortune, boy! It will pay us big."

CHAPTER II

THE TREASURE CHEST

SINCE the Swifts had first known Mr. Wakefield Damon that eccentric character had brought to their attention a number of strange affairs, and some of them had resulted in the betterment of his own and the Swifts' finances. So, no matter how ridiculous his first proposition might sound, Tom and his father were both ready to listen.

A trip to Iceland would scarcely absorb Tom Swift's attention just now, but the fortune Mr. Damon promised him a share of might be a thing not to be scorned. In spite of the inventor's several sources of income and the great sums already invested in the Swift Construction Company and in other well-paying concerns, Tom never saw the time when he could not make good use of more money.

From the time the reader was introduced to "Tom Swift and His Motor Cycle," the title of the first book of this series, down to the twenty-fifth volume, the one preceding this present story,

"Tom Swift and His Electric Locomotive," the young inventor has found good use for much money.

His inventions—some of them marvels as his father intimated—had brought them in much money, it is true. But it "takes money to breed money;" and always this is true as well as trite in the construction and marketing of inventions.

"It takes the cash to put 'em over," Ned Newton, Tom's dearest friend and closest co-worker, was wont to say. "But you scheme 'em out and I'll find the cash."

Newton, who was treasurer of the Swift Construction Company, had faithfully done his part whenever Tom got into a place where he needed money. But here was Mr. Damon with the promise of a "fortune" on which no interest would have to be paid. The young inventor was naturally interested, even though he might be up to his very ears in work.

"That sounds awfully interesting," he said to the blusterous Wakefield Damon. "I don't care much about the ice—unless that is merely figurative—but a fortune—well, what part of Iceland is it in?"

"I don't know," said the visitor bluntly. "But Iceland is not so big a country, is it? Not as big as Australia, for instance, although it is likewise an island."

"You can't walk over it in a day, looking for a fortune," laughed Mr. Swift.

"Don't expect to have to do that," said Mr. Damon, with an answering laugh. "But, bless my calipers! we ought to be able to find Rosestone on the map."

"Is that the name of the place where this fortune is—er—is it buried?" demanded Tom.

"Goodness only knows," said Mr. Damon, tugging at a big wallet and finally getting it out of his inside pocket. "It may be hanging in the air. But the letter comes from Rosestone. I fancy that is a small town. And that is where the fortune is."

"A fortune in what?" asked Mr. Swift.

"A fortune of how much?" demanded Tom.

Mr. Damon blinked his eyes very rapidly. Tom wanted to laugh, for he saw very clearly that their questions were making their friend think. Heretofore he had only been thrilled by the idea of the fortune.

"I declare, Tom Swift! I don't know how much, and I do not know whether the fortune is in money or in stocks and bonds——"

"Or walrus tusks," laughed Tom. "Part of Iceland, I understand, is a pretty savage country, although the people may be peaceable enough."

"Then you know something about Iceland,

Tom Swift? Bless my geographical dictionary! I can't find much about it."

"It is told about in full in the encyclopedia," said Tom. "And it is a country that has always interested me. But I never expect to go to it——"

"Don't say that, Tom Swift! Don't say that!" begged Mr. Damon. "I have got to have your help."

"How do you know there is enough of a fortune to pay two people for going after it?" laughed Tom.

"Here, Damon," said Tom's father, "you are all excited. Sit down here and have a smoke and tell us about it quietly."

The idea of Mr. Wakefield Damon doing anything quietly amused Tom again. But he waited patiently for their friend to compose himself to a degree and tell his story. Like his father, Tom was curious.

"I'll tell you about Aman Dele. I met him a good many years before I ever heard of you Swifts. Quite by accident, too. He was a mystery at first. It was by the strangest chance—or so I always thought—that I came across him. He was a man with a pocket full of money, and he was starving to death."

"Stomach trouble?" asked Mr. Swift shrewdly.

"The money may have been in Russian rubles

and there wasn't enough in his pockets to buy an egg sandwich," chuckled Tom.

"Neither of you is right," said Wakefield Damon, rather gravely for him. "Aman Dele had perfectly good money—Danish money, I found out afterward. I found him in New York where one might think every language in the world is spoken. But he had all the interpreters puzzled."

"And he was a Dane? Why, there is a big Danish colony in New York."

"He was of Danish extraction; but he came from Iceland; and he came from the interior of that island where the people live about as they did when the island was first settled from Denmark, or Norway, or some Scandinavian country."

"Great Scott!" exclaimed Tom suddenly. "That was away back in the time of the Norsemen. Isn't that right, father?"

"It must be," said Mr. Swift, in agreement.

"And you mean that this Aman Dele spoke Old Norse, Mr. Damon?" asked Tom.

"And nothing else. He was just a young fellow and very bashful. He had not entered the country through the Emigration Bureau. He had plenty of money, as I say, and undoubtedly had come across on one of the big ships. Traveling first, or possibly second cabin, his food had been supplied him at the table d'hôte. He had not been obliged to talk. And he did not know a word of French or English, or modern Danish."

"I declare!" exclaimed Mr. Swift. "But money speaks with a louder tongue than anything else! He had money. But it was probably modern Icelandic he spoke, Tom," he added.

"He was both bashful and afraid," said Mr. Damon in answer to Mr. Swift, eagerly reciting his story. "He had tried to talk to people until he was ashamed. And he dared not show his money for fear somebody would get it away from him. He was, as I found out afterward, walking about New York hoping to see some sign familiar to him, or to hear a word of his mother tongue spoken on the street, and growing more and more frightened."

"Fat chance of hearing any Icelandic!" murmured the interested Tom Swift.

"I should say so! I should say so!" agreed Mr. Damon. "And so I thought after I found out what was the matter with the fellow. I saw him lurking in the mouth of an alley right beside a sausage shop. It was over on the lower East Side, and I had just come up from the docks where I had bidden good-bye to some friends who were going to Central America. Almost all the Spigotti boats sailed from the East River docks in those days.

"Well, sir, I saw this young, pale, well-dressed fellow lounging there, and just the look of him interested me. He looked so clean and foreign in his dress, and so out of place. As I watched him, the sausage man came to the door and flung a piece of sausage to a stray dog. The dog grabbed it and ran into the alley. The next moment—bless my links of frankfurters!—this strange fellow grabbed the sausage from the dog and commenced eating it while the disappointed dog ran off howling.

"Did you ever hear of anything so ridiculous? I was stricken stock-still with amazement, myself. Bless my boots! I was stuck right there, staring at the young fellow gnawing on that half spoiled sausage."

"The poor fellow," murmured Mr. Swift.

"That's right. It aroused more than my curiosity. I saw that although he was well dressed and all that, he was starving. I walked right across the street and into the alley and grabbed him," said Mr. Damon.

"He was scared and tried to break away, and even offered me the sausage," continued the narrator. "Guess he thought I was some sort of a policeman. But I was strong in those days and I hung onto him. There was a little coffee shop in sight and I made him go with me there. Just the smell of that rank coffee almost made him

faint. But I made him sip it slowly, and afterward he put away a beefsteak and bread and but-
ter and more coffee. Then his face began to
light up as though there was an electric bulb
turned on inside of his skull."

"Interesting—vastly interesting," commented
Mr. Swift. "But this fortune?"

"I'm coming to it. Give me time," said Mr.
Damon. Then, grinning, he added: "Bless my
pocketbook! you can't expect to get a fortune
in a minute."

"But we hope to hear about the treasure chest
pretty soon," put in Tom.

Mr. Damon selected a paper from several he
took from his wallet. He unfolded it and spread
it out so that both the Swifts could read what
was written on it. It seemed to be the final par-
agraphs of a personal letter to Mr. Damon, and
Tom read aloud:

"* * * So, my dear Mr. Damon, it was always
on our friend's mind that you should see his
country. He had seen the world and he believed
nothing in it was so beautiful and good as Iceland. And Rosestone is the beauty spot of that
beautiful island. You know he has written you
again and again to come here. 'Ah!' he said
to me, his other friend, 'I will bring him at last.
Those Americans are all for business—for the

making of money. It costs a great deal to live in America, and my friend, Damon, may need more than he has now before he dies.'

"So, Mr. Damon, he arranged it this way: His will was made and is proved in our courts. His chest of treasure is waiting for you. But you must come in person and get it. You are to visit his grave before you can have possession of the fortune Aman Dele intended you to have. It is my duty to see that his intentions are fulfilled.

"I hope to see you within the year. I would like to get this responsibility off my mind, for I am an old man and my time may be near. Start at once for Iceland, and let me know when you expect to reach Rosestone.

"Yours in the faith,

"ERICK BRODAK,

"Pastor Rosestone Mission."

CHAPTER III

AMAN DELE

"Now, bless my inmost thoughts! what do you think of that?" Mr. Damon demanded, and burst into another great laugh. "Isn't it a fact that the very strangest things happen to me? I never imagined that day when I fed that starving Icelander that he was rich and would die and leave me a fortune. We were both young men then."

"Why," said Mr. Swift, warmly, "this is wonderful, Damon! It surely is an instance of casting your bread on the waters and getting it back after many days."

"With interest!" chuckled the visitor. "For all I did was to feed Aman Dele and help him find himself——"

"With your usual kindness," broke in Tom, likewise with enthusiasm.

"Tut, tut!" exclaimed Wakefield Damon, with a gesture of dismissal. "Let me tell you more about that Dele. We sat there in the coffee house and stared at each other and neither of us knew how to make the other understand what he wanted to say. But finally I got it in my head that the first thing was to find out where the fellow came from—what part of the world, you know."

"Quite true," murmured Mr. Swift. "That was bright of you."

"Bless my brain-pan! I should say so," cried Mr. Damon, with another laugh. "I grabbed him again and led him to the nearest library. He was more scared than ever, if possible. But I got out a big book of maps and we sat down to look them over. This at last made him know I was a friend.

"Dele couldn't read the names of the countries we looked at; but I knew by his shining eyes that he recognized the shape of some of them. He knew the British Isles. Then we turned the leaves to Sweden and Norway and he began to jabber that strange tongue of his. Then we hit little Denmark, and I was sure we were getting warm," and once more Mr. Damon broke into laughter.

"But we had turned the pages so fast at first that we skipped Greenland and Iceland and Dele kept shaking his head at every country I showed him. But I was sure it must have a close connection with Denmark, wherever his country lay.

So we went back to the beginning and all of a sudden he let out a howl.

"Bless my outlines! he acted tickled to death to see the map of Iceland. Until that time I had had an idea it was as deserted a place as Upper Greenland," went on Mr. Damon. "Well, bless my pocket atlas! I had spotted the land he had come from, I was sure. So I went to the librarian and told him the fix I was in and he actually guessed that Dele was one of those folk who talked like the old Norsemen—like Eric the Red, and Leif Ericksen, and those other Norsemen who swept the seas clean in the old days.

"So we found a couple of books with passages printed in them in Old Norse. When Dele saw them he was tickled pink. He read them as though they were the last edition of the sporting extra!" and Mr. Damon began to laugh once more.

"Bless my antiques! but it seemed to me he was as far behind the times as the rudder of Noah's ark."

"What did you do with him?" asked Mr. Barton Swift, much amused.

"Well, you know, I couldn't turn him adrift. Besides, by that time we had learned to understand each other a little by signs. I borrowed the books and we took them to my rooms. In a few days I had learned half a dozen Icelandic

words (I've forgotten 'em all now) and Aman
Dele had learned how to order ham and eggs
and a cup of coffee in restaurant English," and
Damon went off into another loud burst of
laughter.

"So we got on pretty well. And by and by
he showed me the money he carried. And then,
bless my pocketbook, I *was* bowled over! I,
thinking he was as poor as a church mouse all
the time! Bless my exchange! When we got
that Danish money turned into American coin of
the realm, it seemed he had thousands of dollars."

"That *was* an experience," commented Tom's
father.

"Yes, indeed. He stayed with me until he
learned to know the ropes and could speak fair
English. He traveled all over the country and
came back to visit me again. He was urgent that
I should go to Iceland with him. Said there
was no part of America as fine as the place he
lived. He objected to the States because we
didn't have reindeer pulling our street cars instead of horses. This was before the age of the
trolley, you know.

"Bless my antlers! wouldn't that have looked
fine? Cars dragged by reindeer! Well, I could
not go home with him, and all through these years
he has written me, off and on, to try to get me
to take the journey to his little home town. Now

he's left me this fortune. But, you see, he's fixed it so that I must finally visit his home if I am to enjoy his legacy."

"That is awfully interesting, Mr. Damon. But why don't you go right along and get the treasure chest alone?" Tom asked.

"Bless my brassbound luggage!" cried Mr. Damon. "Go alone to Iceland? I don't believe I could ever find it!"

The Swifts laughed at that joke; but Tom continued to shake his head. And it was a most decided shake, at that.

"Iceland is perfectly civilized. The only danger you run is being cheated by hotel keepers and travelers' agents."

"But, Tom, the treasure!"

"You don't even know how much it is," chuckled the young inventor. "Perhaps it isn't large enough to divide in half even! It maybe won't pay you for going alone, let alone paying me. And I'm a sight too busy to go so far away from Shopton right now."

"I'll guarantee you that the treasure is a big one. How much will you want to leave what you are doing and go with me?" demanded their strange friend, with much earnestness.

"I tell you it can't be done!" and Tom continued to wag his head negatively.

"You've got something so important that you

cannot possibly go with me?" It was plain that Mr. Wakefield Damon was going to be vastly disappointed.

"Perhaps. Father and I were just talking over a scheme that greatly interests me, I admit. But there is another thing that stays me at this time. Mr. Nestor—perhaps you have heard it?—is very ill. I would not want to go away now. You know, Mary Nestor would feel—rightly so, I think—that I was neglecting her if I left for Iceland at this time."

"Bless my doctor's book!" growled the disappointed Mr. Damon. "What is the matter with all the doctors nowadays? Don't any of them know enough to help Mary's father? I was over to see him myself last week. Looks to me as though the medicos were just experimenting with him. I'm thankful to say I seldom have any need for medicine or doctors."

"I fancy the physicians are puzzled about Mr. Nestor's case," said Mr. Barton Swift thoughtfully. "But they have sent for a specialist to come up from New York. We may learn shortly more about what is the matter with him. This New York doctor has had wonderful success. They say the cures he has to his credit are almost miraculous."

Mr. Damon looked rather gloomy. But he expressed sympathy for Mary's father.

"He's a fine man. I wish him well. But I'm mighty sorry if his sickness stands in the way of your going with me, Tom," he grumbled.

"Oh, I might find other reasons, too," declared Tom, smiling.

"Bless my pocketbook, Tom! name your own price," cried his eccentric friend.

"It can't be done, I tell you. You go on to Iceland. When you get back I may have something to show you that you will agree was quite worth my while."

Even to Mr. Damon the young inventor was not ready to talk about his plans for the flying boat that so engrossed his mind. The visitor remained to dinner; but Tom did not once mention this particular topic which he had been discussing with his father previous to Mr. Damon's appearance.

The latter, seeing he could not have his way with his young friend in the matter of the voyage to Iceland, did not sulk. As usual he cheerfully—and noisily—discussed plans for the voyage, blessing almost everything and everybody that might be connected with the proposed journey.

"I shall start next week, go to Denmark, and from there take ship to Iceland. I've found out already that is the way to do. But I hate traveling alone, as you both know. And I shall want to get back again as soon as possible, for I am curious about this new thing you are studying about, Tom. Will it be a land, water, or air marvel?"

But Tom refused to be drawn into any discussion at all about his idea. "Wait!" was all he would say to his old friend.

CHAPTER IV

A HELPING HAND

Tom Swift, as has been said, did not overlook the value of money and the good uses to which it might be put. But he did not think that he wanted any share in Mr. Wakefield Damon's venture after the mysterious treasure chest that had been left to him in the interior areas of Iceland. He was telling Mary Nestor about it that evening as he was driving her in his electric runabout through the suburbs of Shopton and out into the country.

If Tom did not go after her and actually insist upon the girl's taking a frequent ride with him, Mary would scarcely have had "a sniff of the open air," as her mother told her. They were both much engaged in caring for Mr. Nestor, whose disease at this time evaded the diagnoses of all the physicians who had attended him.

With Mary, as well as with his father and Ned Newton, Tom usually discussed the most secret plans regarding his inventions; so, besides telling Mary about Mr. Damon's odd predicament, he likewise spoke of his hope of building a better flying boat than had as yet been perfected. Some of his ideas upon this subject were not new to the girl.

"I believe you will achieve a really wonderful thing, Tom," she told him, with enthusiasm. "But it will be a monster—bigger than your great airship that you sold the Government."

"I am not sure about those details as yet," Tom said, shaking his head and looking sharply ahead, for the dusk was gathering fast. "The idea is just milling in my mind. Yet, I confess, I have had Ned Newton do a little figuring for me—especially regarding the getting of estimates for certain parts. Our shops cannot turn out every part of such a craft any more than we could build all of the electric locomotive we sold to the Hendrickton and Pas Alos Railroad."

"Aren't you afraid, Tom," Mary asked doubtfully, "to trust outside people with your plans that way? Somebody in some other shop may steal your ideas."

He shook his head, smiling. "No, no. I never trust my plans in full to any of the construction-works people. I may have my wings built in one shop, the cabin-boat in another, or the prow in a third. And, of course, we shall buy the motors outright. No, no. An invention is like a doctor's prescription. When it is put together it

takes a pretty good analyst to discover the ingre-
dients. And the parts of an invention have to
be assembled by the mind that dreamed out the
whole contraption."

"Dear me," sighed Mary, "I wish some doctor had a prescription that would help father."

"I wish so, too!" cried Tom heartily. "When
does the specialist arrive?"

"Dr. Raddiker?"

"Is that his name?"

"Yes. Some kind of a foreigner. A very
learned man, I believe," Mary said, with rising
confidence. "What Dr. Goslap tells mother and
me about him encourages us vastly. Dr. Raddiker is a great diagnostician."

"Wonder what sort of a doctor this fellow
needs who is coming along the road?" demanded
Tom suddenly. "He'll have that car climbing
the telephone poles next."

"Goodness, Tom!" cried Mary, likewise seeing
the eccentrically acting car ahead of them, and
evidently heading for Shopton. "He'll have it in
the ditch next."

"Great Scott!" shouted Tom. "That's exactly
where he has got it!"

At that moment the car ahead backed around
into the hedge on one side of the highway and
then shot across the road and plunged, nose-first,
into the deep ditch on the other side, which was

here undefended by a railing. Tom and Mary heard a wild shout for "Hellup!" and then an explosion of phrases that the young inventor was glad were uttered in some foreign tongue, for he feared that they were not polite enough for Mary's ear.

Tom Swift speeded up his runabout and they reached the scene of the accident just as the awkward chauffeur was crawling out of the mud. The nose of the car was buried in the mire and the occupant of the tonneau of the car was struggling with the door while he ejaculated in broken English:

"Hellup! Why for did I let such a dumbskull drive de car? Ach! I should be shot for my foolishness, undt he should be hung for inefficiency. Yah! Hellup!"

Mary hopped out of Tom's car quickly and ran to help the excited stranger open the door of the closed car. But Tom turned his attention to the chauffeur. Nothing could be done for the car itself, he saw at a glance, on its own power.

"Hi!" Tom shouted to the fellow in the ditch. "Go back and shut off your engine. She is heading for China right now. Want her to go there?"

"She can go to perdition for all of me!" grumbled the mud-covered chauffeur. "She's got the Old Boy in her."

"For vy you call it me names?" demanded the

passenger, indignantly, just then bursting out of
the motor-car. He was a bushy-headed man
with owl-like spectacles and evidently the pos-
sessor of a querulous temper. "He is most in-
sulting! Undt he is the worst driver I ever had.
Dumbskull!"

"You're the Old Boy, all right, but not the one
I meant was in that engine," growled the chauffeur sullenly. "You are a crazy nuisance——"

Tom had got out, reached the head of the car,
and by leaning down the ditch side with care,
he shut off the thumping engine. He now swung
to look at the muttering chauffeur. The latter
was ill-favored of feature and betrayed frankly
that his mental condition had been brought about
by indulgence in liquor.

"You work for Peltin Brothers, at Norwalk,"
Tom said sharply. "I've seen you before. This
car from their garage?"

"He comes from it, the Norwalk garage," interposed the strange man who was now rescuing
sundry bundles and bags from the interior of the
car. "The car, it is mine. My other driver leaf
me in one lurch, you say, no? This fellow—
ah-ha! He is a low-life. It is not gasoline he
buy for the car, but bad whisky for himself."

"Well, you are in a bad mess," Tom said to
the driver. "Come on and let's see what we can
do about getting her up on the road."

The man shook his head vigorously. He backed away, up the side of the ditch. When he reached the sound road he started right away from there, only looking back over his shoulder to bawl:

"I wouldn't help that crazy guy, or touch that car, for a farm down east with a pig on't. You can have it, for all o' me!"

"Well!" exclaimed Mary, in disgust.

"A fine dog that!" grumbled Tom ruefully.

"A dumbskull!" ejaculated the strange gentleman, standing amid his baggage.

"Why! How mean!" cried Mary.

"Where were you going, sir?" Tom Swift asked.

"To a place called Shopton. Do you know it?"

"We live there," said the young inventor briskly. "It is not far. If nobody else comes along, the young lady will drive you in my runabout. I will stay until help comes for the car. Or, maybe, we can get it out of the mud ourselves."

"Ach! Not me!" cried the stranger. "I must not soil or injure my hands. I do not lift weights. I am not here to strain my muscles and rack my nerves for such things as this. Ach, no!"

Tom and Mary stared at each other. They did not know whether to be amused or disgusted with the stranger. He seemed willing enough to accept help, but he was not inclined to help himself!

"Well," Tom said finally, and dryly, "you don't mind if I try to recover your car for you?"

"Not at all," declared the man, with a shrug. "You will do what you please. But I, I do not aid."

"But it is your car? You bought and paid for it?"

"Yes, yes! What has that to do with it? I know my place. It is not working in the muddy ditch over a motor-car. No!"

"I believe you," muttered Tom to Mary. "His place is somewhere on a mantelpiece for an ornament."

"Hush, Tom," the girl said. "Will you help him?"

"For my own satisfaction, not because I am inclined to play the Samaritan to such a fellow. I'll lend the helping hand."

CHAPTER V

WHAT CAME OF IT

QUEERLY as this man acted, Tom Swift could not have left either him or his car on the road and in the lurch. He would have felt himself to be as mean as the half intoxicated chauffeur from the Norwalk garage.

Besides, the young fellow knew without her telling him that Mary would expect him to do all he could in the emergency, and Mary's opinion was, of course, of the first importance to Tom. While the stranger sat on the bank of the ditch with his baggage about him, not offering to lift his hand to aid, the young inventor planned and put into execution a method of rescuing the mired automobile.

He had a small ax in the tool box of the electric runabout. With this he cut a green, tough sapling about as big around as his shank. This he used to pry the nose of the stranger's motor-car out of the mud.

He used the pry to break down the edge of the

ditch, too, and finally he used a couple of non-skid chains to tackle the two cars together, and with the power of his own machine, used very skilfully, he finally dragged the other car to the highway.

Meanwhile the owner of that car sat placidly, smoking little, strong-smelling cigarettes which he rolled himself with dextrous fingers, and watched the work quite impersonally. Mary disapproved of cigarettes in any case and she whispered to Tom that she didn't know but she was sorry that she had urged him to help the strange man!

"Ach! Brawn is not to be scorned," said the man, when the motor-car stood upon its four wheels on the road. "It is not so good like brains—no, no. But if one has not the brains and the learning, it is well to be a mechanic, yes?"

Mary grew rosy-red at that. She considered it an insult to Tom Swift. She might have said something sharp, but her friend interposed, with a grin:

"They say that a man with brains alone on a desert island will live where a dull man, possessing only strength, would die. But I bet a stupid man with good muscles will live better in the haunts of civilization than a penniless man of brains. What would you do if you had been marooned here without money and nobody to help you?"

"Ach! You are, perhaps, a philosopher?" grumbled the man.

"You don't have to possess much book education to be that," laughed Tom. "Well, sir, you get in the runabout with the young lady. She can drive. I'll try to bring your car along behind. Where are you stopping in Shopton?" he added, as the man began to gather his various bags and bundles and pack them into the runabout until there was scarcely room for the girl to reach the pedals with her feet.

"Is there not a hotel, no?"

"The Shopton House. A commercial hotel."

"I will try it. This is one vacation. I have but one thing to do while I am avay from New York. I need the change and fresh air, or I vould never come to a place like this in answer to any call. No!"

"I wonder what and who he is," thought Tom Swift, as Mary finally started the runabout and he, himself, climbed into the other car.

The car had been pretty well shaken up by its plunge into the ditch; and the engine balked several times before Tom managed to get it to town. Therefore Mary got far ahead of him with the car's owner.

When Tom Swift got to the Shopton House

he found his electric runabout standing at the curb. Mary had gone home, for it was now quite late in the evening. Tom ran the shaken car to the nearest garage and then went into the hotel to leave word for the stranger where his property could be found.

"You just had a guest come in, didn't you?" Tom asked the clerk.

The latter began to grin. "You mean the foreign feller?"

"Some kind of a Dutchman, I guess," said the young inventor. "What's his name?"

"Look on the book and see," was the reply. "I can't read it, and I don't know what to call him. He not only speaks broken English, but he writes broken English."

"Really?" responded Tom, with a laugh. "Let's take a squint at it."

He wheeled the register about on its swivel and peered at the crabbed writing. He could read "NewYork,U.S.of Amerika." But the name of the man looked as much like a hen track as it did like anything written in the English language.

"He's one of these foreign musicians, I bet," said the clerk to Tom. "And he wanted a room with a bath and hot running water!"

"There isn't anything like that in this house," answered Tom, with a laugh.

"If there was, I'd rent it myself," declared the other. "He sniffed a lot about 'de pad accommodations'; but he's staying the night. Want to see him?"

"No. I've seen enough of him, to tell the truth," said Tom. "But you'd better get word to him where his car is. And don't tell him anything about me! I don't want him hunting me up and either thanking me or trying to pay me."

But secretly Tom did not believe the queer stranger would ever consider it necessary to thank those who had helped him out of his difficulty.

"He's one more Dutchman with a swelled head," was the young inventor's private comment, as he drove his runabout home.

It was too late to go to Mary's house again. But in the morning, the first thing when he reached his private office, he called the Nestor house. Mrs. Nestor answered the call and Tom knew, by her voice, that she was much disturbed.

"The doctors were here for a consultation again early this morning, Tom," the woman said brokenly. "They seem to have very little hope that Mr. Nestor will ever be better. And they have given up hope of the specialist's coming——"

"You mean the Dr. Raddiker Mary was speaking of?" asked Tom quickly.

"Yes. They expected him yesterday. They

find he has left New York for a vacation and, being such a busy man, he probably will not come here to consult with our doctors on a single case. They give us no hope——"

"Oh! Don't say that, Mrs. Nestor!" Tom interrupted.

"It is the way we both feel," said Mary's mother. "If I knew of any diagnostician or specialist whom we could secure, no matter what it costs, I would ask you to get him here, Tom."

"Wait!" cried Tom suddenly. "I'm coming over. There must be some way——"

He hung up without finishing his sentence. To tell the truth he had no idea how to help Mrs. Nestor and Mary. But it seemed to him that it was almost brutal just to remain idle while the sick man slowly lost strength and vitality.

He had intended giving his entire attention that day to considering plans for the flying boat that he was determined to build. But his fears for Mr. Nestor and his sympathy for Mary and her mother would not allow of that.

He pulled down the roller-top of his desk again and started out of the shops. He had no idea what he could do to help; and yet milling about in his brain there was a hazy idea that there *must* be something which could be done to aid Mary's father.

If that Dr. Raddiker had only come to con-

sult upon the case! Mary had spoken of him
so hopefully. Dr. Raddiker. Another of these
crazy foreigners, perhaps——

The thought of the unreadable writing on the
Shopton House register the evening before suddenly stabbed Tom Swift's brain like a ray of
light in the darkness. He said afterward that
his mind seemed to be suddenly lit up by a star-
tling thought.

He started on a run for downtown, not even
waiting to get out the car.

CHAPTER VI

THE PRONOUNCEMENT

THE clerk of the Shopton House with whom
Tom had talked the previous evening was standing in the doorway, grinning widely. He hailed
the younger fellow before the latter could put his
first question:

"Hey, there, Swift! Looking for the Great
Unknown?"

"That foreigner? Yes. Is he here?" demanded Tom.

"Just gone. Couldn't stand us any longer. We
don't know how to make coffee as they make it
in some place he called Vienna. There's no
Vienna in this state."

"He means Vienna, Austria. Did he start for
that place before breakfast?"

"Well, maybe. Anyway, he got the boy to cart
all his truck over to the garage. He is going to
leave town at once."

"Not much he won't, if he's the man I think
he is!" exclaimed Tom, under his breath, and he

started for the garage. "I ought to have guessed it last night."

The motor-car Tom had rescued on the road had been repaired and was now standing by the curb. Its owner had hired another driver to take him on his way. Big spectacles and all, the stranger was planted in the back seat with his goods and chattels around him. He welcomed Tom Swift with a sort of sour smile.

"They tell me you are an inventor and a young man of property, yes—no?" began the peculiar man. "So it would be to insult you to offer you pay for what you did for me last evening. Yes?"

"You can insult me by offering money, all right," answered Tom. "But I mean to exact payment for helping you."

"Ach! Yes? Indeed? And how shall I pay you?"

"You are Dr. Raddiker!" exclaimed the young fellow.

"For sure. Dr. Simon Raddiker. Undt I mean to get away from this place soon. What is your bill?"

"You came up here to consult with some doctors upon a case that is puzzling them, did you not?"

"Not at all! Not at all!" cried the other. "I am on one vacation. I am in no mood to consult mit dese country doctors. Ach! For why should I work when it is a vacation I need?"

"But think of the sick man!" cried Tom almost angrily. "Suppose he needs you?"

"I do not know that. I know nothing about it yet. Why should I consider him?" and the scientist shrugged his shoulders. "What is he to me?"

"He's a good deal to me," declared Tom Swift sternly. "You must pay me for helping you out last night by seeing this man—Mr. Nestor."

"Not so! Not so!" cried Dr. Raddiker, his eyes flashing behind his huge spectacles. "Ach! You are like one of these American bandits—yes? You say you will take what you want if I will not give it cheerfully, yes? Ach!"

"That is the only way you can pay your bill," declared Tom.

"Then the bill, it goes unpaid," Raddiker almost snarled at him. To the driver of the car he added: "Go on! I haf enough of this town. I never want to see it again."

The querulous, nervous, excited savant was doubtless an unhappy soul, and he liked to make other people unhappy. He turned about as the car started and cried:

"Gif my regards to the young lady. She was very nice and friendly yet. She is the only nice person I meet since I come from New York."

"Hold on!" commanded Tom. He leaped upon the running board and leaned over and stopped the car in spite of the chauffeur. His eyes flashed into those of the remarkable Dr. Raddiker.

"Hold on!" he repeated. "You speak of that girl. Do you know who she is? It is her father who is dying and whom the doctors here want you to visit. Can't you do that much for the poor girl who was nice to you?"

"You are telling me the truth—yes?" stammered Raddiker doubtfully.

"Tell this man to drive you to Mr. Nestor's house. His daughter will be there," the young fellow replied.

"Vell! Vell!" agreed Raddiker. "Go on. We will try. But if you deceive me—Ach!"

He was evidently very angry. Tom did not care how angry the man was with him; he was determined he should fulfill his agreement with the local doctors and examine Mr. Nestor.

Tom rode beside the chauffeur and the moment the car stopped at the Nestor place he called Mary to the door and ran in himself and had Mrs. Nestor call up the two doctors who had been attending her husband.

Dr. Raddiker put the best face he could on a troublesome matter, now that he saw Mary and knew that the patient was one in whom she had an interest. Mary had quite charmed the grouchy savant. He stamped into the house with one of his small bags, peering about through his huge spectacles, and apparently criticising unfavorably everything that he saw.

It was certain that he criticised everything the doctors in the case had done and bluntly told them his small opinion of them when they arrived in haste to meet him. But they knew Raddiker and his unpleasant manners and accepted his diatribes in silence. One of the local physicians afterward told Tom that he considered a man with as keen a mind as the foreign doctor had the right to be as ungentlemanly as he pleased.

"Not a bit!" cried the young inventor. "The greatest man in the world could not be excused for using such language or displaying such a mean spirit."

However, in the matter of Mr. Nestor's illness, the famous Dr. Raddiker did his work well, being pressed to it by the circumstances. Had it not been for Tom Swift he would have gone away disgruntled from Shopton and refused to see the invalid.

But, as was the nature of the strange man, having once questioned the other physicians and gained a full history of the case, he became interested. And once he was interested in a puzzling problem, Dr. Raddiker hung on to it like a bull-dog to a bone!

He would not allow them to remove his automobile from before the door, and it remained in readiness for departure. He was in just as much haste as ever to leave the despised Shopton. But he stayed beside Mr. Nestor's bed for twelve hours, watching him, studying the fluctuating symptoms of the disease, and finally late that night was ready to give his diagnosis.

Having scolded the other doctors and having declared that no medicine could aid the patient, Dr. Raddiker left to continue his "vacation" after making a most strange pronouncement regarding the case. When Tom Swift heard of it the next day he was inclined to believe that the savant was quite as mad as he appeared to be.

"What's that?" he cried. "You don't mean he said *that*, Mary? That your father must go to the Arctic? The man is mad! Maybe he expects him to join some party in search of the Pole? Don't tell me that fellow is a scientist! He has escaped from a madhouse!"

But the physician had been serious. A change of climate was all that would save Mr. Nestor. And a change to a very cold climate was the change that would be most efficacious.

The local doctors were quite serious about it. The disease from which Mr. Nestor suffered, when once named by Raddiker, was recognized as a rare but well understood trouble. A few weeks in a climate of keen frost might entirely eradicate the germs of the disease that had stricken Mary's father.

The treatment had been pointed out. To say "change of climate" was all very well. But as Mary confessed to Tom, the way for such a change seemed closed. Who was to go with Mr. Nestor on any such journey?

He could not go alone. Mrs. Nestor was in such health herself that the physicians would not recommend such a journey for her. In fact, they forbade thought of it. Mary could not leave her mother.

"Besides, father could not be burdened with a girl," she confessed to Tom Swift. "He should have no responsibilities upon his mind but the recovery of his own health. That Raddiker! He told us just enough to stir us all up and add to our worriments. He told us how father might be aided to health, but he does not point out the way for us to bring it about. I declare, Tom, neither mother nor I has the first idea of what we ought to do!"

CHAPTER VII

A GOOD DEAL ON HIS MIND

Tom came around by the slaughter house at the railroad switch, on the far edge of Shopton, on his way home from the Nestor house. He knew several of the men who worked there, and he wanted something that could only be supplied in the vicinity of the town at that place.

"Pigs' bladders? The land sake! What for, Mister Tom?" demanded Harry M'Connel, the man the young inventor asked. "You ain't makin' no contraption for to make pigs fly, are you, now? The price of pork has gone up high enough already."

"I'm not so sure that the bladders may not help me scheme out something that will aid man to fly," laughed Tom Swift.

"You shall have the bladders," declared M'Connel. "But I never mean to go up in one of them flying machines myself. Still and all, there's some folks I'd just as lief would go scootin' skyward as not, and I hope if they do they never

48

come down again," added the slaughter-house man, grumblingly.

He went outside, selected a pair of good-sized pigs' bladders, washed them, and brought them back to the young inventor. Tom thanked him and went home with the bladders. When a little boy he used to get these bladders for balloons. He blew them up now in the same way, tied them, and hung them out of his bedroom window to dry, warning Rad and Koku to let them alone.

"Master make great medicine with them," the giant declared to Rad Sampson. "Make wonder! Whoo!"

"Yo' make me sick—whoo!" muttered old Rad. "What kind of med'cine you think can be made out o' a pig's bladder, big man? You is sho'-nuff crazy."

But Koku remembered what the magicians and medicine men did with such receptacles in his own country and shook his head. He held Tom Swift quite as able to make black magic as any medicine man who ran half naked in the wilds.

"You see!" he declared earnestly. "Master make big noise. Do wunnerful thing. Mighty smart."

"Which *you* isn't," declared Eradicate with scorn. "I dunno what Mist' Swift and Mars' Tom wants yo' round yere for, anyway. Yo' ain't a smitch o' good, as I can see. Yo' ain't even to be trusted to peel spuds. I haf to peel de peels after you."

"Koku great chief. He cannot do woman's work."

"Hey!" cried old Rad. "Since you got dat checkered suit out West dere, whar Mars' Tom took his electric engine, dere ain't been any holdin' yo'. Makes yo' too uppity to wear good clo'es. A breech-clout an' a string of beads is de best yo' knowed about dressin' 'fore yo' come here."

Koku showed his teeth at that, and stalked away. He liked to exercise authority about the house and the shops; but Rad had been here long before Koku, and he would not endure any usurpation in the control of even small things.

When there was no subject of controversy between them, however, the two were very good friends. The giant often shouldered burdens for Rad and said nothing about it. And he never took one of his wild jaunts through the countryside about Shopton that he did not bring back to Rad some treasure, or present—often of a laughter-provoking nature.

Both Rad and Koku loved to go fishing at Lake Carlopa, and two mornings later they stole away after breakfast with tackle and bait for the near shore of the lake. They went to a favorite strip of low bank, hidden by hazel brush from observation except from the open lake, and cast for white perch which were known to be plentiful at this spot.

At first the perch were shy and Koku began to mutter charms to entice them.

"Hey! Yo' call dat Voodoo talk?" grumbled Rad, who was religious himself and did not approve of "no heathen jabber." "Yo' stop dat, Koku! De good Lawd'll send some kind of a big fish—a eel, mebbe—an' tangle you all up an' swaller yo' alibe. Huh! I got a bite. See dere, big man. I's got it! Not you, you ole—— Woof!"

For what he jerked ashore when he thought the fish was well hooked was a rotten snag. Koku was busy himself with a nibble just then or he might have angered his old friend by laughing. He might also have driven all the fish away, for when Koku laughed he could be heard for half a mile at least!

"What yo' got, boy?" asked the disgruntled Rad Sampson. "A rubber boot?"

But Koku had caught a fine, shining perch and he began dancing around the tiny enclosed lawn in great delight.

"Stop dat ghost-dancing!" exclaimed Rad. "String dat fish on dat withe. Dat's only de fust one. Mars' Tom hisself can eat a dozen ob dem for his supper."

"Sh!" hissed Koku suddenly, putting up a great hand in warning.

He had landed on one splay foot and he stood there, with the other one raised, bent forward and listening. He had heard something beyond the hazel hedge. As Rad often said, Koku ought to possess the most wonderful hearing—his ears were big enough!

In a moment he crept toward the repeated sound, his movements as soundless as those of a hunting cat. Rad came close behind him, trying to suppress a rather asthmatic breath and stepping as though he were walking on eggs. The sound was repeated—a little splashing.

Through an opening in the brush Rad suddenly caught sight of a moving object. He grabbed Koku's bare and hairy wrist.

"Hold hard, big man!" he gasped. "Dat's a bear!"

They were almost within stone's throw of civilization, and there had not been a bear heard of in that part of the State for fifty years; nevertheless, Rad was convinced of the presence of Bruin.

"A bear?" muttered the giant, not quite sure what the word meant. His knowledge of anything but the commonest English terms was meagre.

The thing beyond the bushes moved. It was down beside the lake itself, and Rad was sure it must be drinking.

"Yo' look out, giant!" he whispered warningly to the giant.

But there was nothing much that Koku was really afraid of save spirits and magic. Any animal smaller than an elephant or rhinoceros he was not much afraid to attack. He uttered a challenging yell, leaped almost straight up in the air, and went over the hedge of hazel brush as though from a spring-board.

It is fortunate he did not land upon Eradicate Sampson's "bear." That individual likewise uttered a yell and leaped away from the giant with much agility.

"Whoo! Ketch him!" shouted Eradicate, charging through the bushes. "Don't let him git away, boy!"

But the giant remained rooted where he had landed upon the sandy beach. Almost at his feet, floating on the surface of the quiet water, was a polished piece of hollow bamboo to which a pair of inflated bladders was attached—one on either side of the stick.

"Mars' Tom!" shrieked Eradicate Sampson.

"Master no bear—what you say!" exclaimed Koku angrily. "Koku jump on him, he be all smashed up. Rad old fool!"

"Hey!" cried Tom Swift, with some heat. "You big clown! Don't be so quick to jump on anything or anybody. Even a bear has some rights that you are bound to respect. And you, Rad, why did you sic him onto me?"

"Nebber did such a thing!" declared Rad warmly. "Nobody but a big fool giant would try to jump right down a bear's throat widout lookin' whar he was jumpin'! Huh!"

Koku likewise snorted his disgust. As usual, the two tried to lay the fault on each other. But Tom came back with a grin on his face.

"I certainly did think a flying pterodactyl, or something of the kind, was swooping over those bushes to get me," he declared.

"He's sure wuss nor dat," declared Rad solemnly. "He's wuss nor a terrydicktil—sure is. He's wuss dan a locofoco."

Koku rolled his eyes tremendously at the sound of these big words which he no more understood than Rad himself did. Tom hastened to relieve the giant's feelings to a degree.

"How many fish did you boys catch?" he asked.

"All lak' Mist' Damon cotched when he went to Florida after tarpon. One!" chuckled Rad. "Mist' Damon said he was two days cotchin' dat one; an' when he seen how big it was he thought he ought t've spent a week at it. This

Koku actin' like it was de on'y fish ever caught in dis lake," he added, with scorn.

"Well, go on, you two, with your fishing," said Tom. "I've a problem to think out and I don't want to be bothered by either pterodactyls or locofocos. Get along now."

He plumped himself down on the sand again and fixed his gaze upon the bobbing piece of bamboo and the inflated bladders. Tom had known, without his father's declaration to that effect, that one of the chief problems he had to solve in the matter of building a better flying boat than anybody else was the problem of constructing his invention so that it could settle in a rough sea without being capsized.

The puzzling thought was with him, day and night. It ran in his head like a tune that sometimes seems to fill one's mind to the expulsion of everything else. Yet, when the young inventor was left alone again and tried to settle himself to his problem in statics, his thought weaved a pattern something like this:

"A shell of some light metal—aluminum, we'll say—buoyed on the outside by additional air chambers. Humph, it would look extremely awkward. But, as Mr. Nestor says very often, the look of a thing isn't what counts. Poor Mr. Nestor! What will those two women do if he does not live?

"How about double walls from stem to stern for air chambers? Humph! Bless my blown-up bladders! as Mr. Damon might say," and he chuckled. "Mr. Damon catching a tarpon so big that he thought he should have spent a week landing it. Humph!

"And he starts in a day or two for Iceland. Br-r-r! That's one cold country, I bet! Cold! Iceland! Why, if Mr. Nestor went there for a few weeks—Great Scott!" exclaimed Tom Swift, suddenly rising and forgetting all about his bamboo stick and pigs' bladders floating on the lake.

"What have I been thinking of? Wakefield Damon is just the man for us!"

He started away from the lake at top speed, forgetting for the time all about his plans for a flying boat that would astonish the world.

CHAPTER VIII

THE EXPEDITION SETS OFF

Tom Swift was quite sure that Mr. Wakefield Damon had not been up from Waterfield since the specialist had diagnosed Mr. Nestor's trouble, and probably had not heard of Dr. Raddiker's advice. The last Tom had heard from his eccentric friend, he was making preparations to leave for New York very shortly.

The young inventor did not even halt at the house to tell his father what he purposed doing; but he got out his electric runabout and made as good time as the town speed ordinance allowed to Mary Nestor's house.

Mary and her mother were in no more cheerful state of mind than they had been when Tom had last seen them. They had canvassed all the possible ways they could think of to bring about the desired trip for Mr. Nestor into the North, but had accomplished nothing.

"Every way seems shut by a door that is barred and locked, Tom," sighed Mary to her sympathetic friend. "We do not know what to do."

"Put on your hat and jacket and come for a ride," proposed the young fellow.

"But that won't help father," she complained. "And I ought not to take you from your work and let you drive me about the country. It isn't right."

"The trouble with you, Mary," said Tom, grinning, "more than anything else, is your New England conscience. Don't worry about what is right so much. Come on. I have a reason for taking you for a ride to-day."

When they were on the road and she knew that he was heading for Waterfield and Mr. Damon's house she expressed satisfaction. She was fond of Mr. Damon, and that eccentric gentleman was fond of Mary.

"But I feel condemned, Tom, when I go around to see people and talk and laugh—as one will—and then remember that father is so poorly and that there seems so little chance of his ever recovering his health."

"Do you believe that Raddiker knew what he was talking about?"

"I do, indeed. The other doctors have much confidence in him. He is a wonderful scientist. They say they wonder why he came over here when he was so successful and so much admired for his knowledge in Austria."

"I know why he came," grumbled Tom, who could not bring himself to like Dr. Raddiker after his experience with him. "The same reason that all those foreigners come over here. A million kronen is worth about two cents of our money. And then they say that Americans are so mercenary!"

"Well, it does not seem that his pointing out the trouble with father is going to help save him," sighed Mary.

"Don't be too sure about that," rejoined Tom with a change of tone. "Here is Mr. Damon's place. Look at the trunks and packing boxes on the porch. Does he intend to take all those with him to Denmark?"

There seemed to be a wonderful amount of stir around the Damon premises. Mrs. Damon, who had long since ceased to interfere when her husband got the wanderlust, sat placidly in a rocking chair and weaved back and forth, knitting. She was the only calm looking object around the place, for even the hens were running and squawking in the yard as Mr. Damon's serving man darted back and forth, subject to his employer's call.

"Bless my spring-heel boots!" ejaculated Mr. Damon, rushing out to greet the two visitors. "Time is flying and I am so busy that I can't think of half the things I want to do before my departure for New York. I was afraid I should not see either of you young folks again——

"Bless my optic nerve, Mary! how sweet you are looking. Isn't she, Mrs. Damon? Won't you both get out?"

"I will," said Mary promptly, taking her cue from Tom Swift's look. "I must talk to Mrs. Damon."

"Do so—do so," cried the gentleman. "Maybe she will answer you; but I don't often get a reply from her," and he burst into one of his laughs. "Bless my wagging tongue! She says she does not get a chance to say a word until I am run down."

He saw instantly that Tom had something serious on his mind. Mr. Damon was not at all an unobservant man. He whispered when Mary had run up the path to the porch:

"What's the matter, Tom, my boy? Is Nestor worse?"

"I don't know that he is. But they have had the consultation with the foreign doctor."

"With that specialist?"

"Yes. He came to Shopton. A funny fellow, but the other doctors think he knows all about Mr. Nestor's complaint."

"What is it?" demanded Mr. Damon. "A very queer case! Bless my thermometer, a very queer case!"

"As far as I can see," grumbled Tom Swift, "it is just as queer now—or queerer—than it was before Dr. Raddiker came."

"Ah-ha!" ejaculated Mr. Damon. "The famous Dr. Raddiker, the European scientist? Bless my medical dictionary! he is a wonderful man."

"Yes? Well, maybe. But he has exploded a regular medical bomb in the Nestor household. He says the only sure cure for Mr. Nestor's complaint is for him to leave home."

"Change of climate, Tom?"

"Very much so. The temperature isn't right for him here. He has got to go where the quicksilver takes a toboggan to the bottom of the glass."

"Bless my thermostat! You don't mean——?"

"That is it, exactly," Tom assured him. "Dr. Raddiker declared the only cure for this disease is a cold climate—a much colder climate than ours. And that Mr. Nestor will have to remain in that colder climate for several weeks, if not months. Now, you know that Mrs. Nestor could never stand such an experience. Her bronchial trouble would be aggravated."

"Well, well!"

"Mr. Nestor cannot go alone. Her mother would never feel comfortable an hour if Mary went with him, even to the North Cape, for instance. It is not to be thought of."

"Bless my chilblains!" interrupted Mr. Damon excitedly. "If it is a cold country he needs, and all that, what could be finer than Iceland?"

"At least," chuckled Tom Swift, "the name of that island is most suggestive."

"And from all I have managed to learn, for a good part of the year it is cold enough up there to satisfy the most critical polar bear."

"True for you."

"He's going with me, Tom, if he can travel. Of course he will!" cried Mr. Damon, jumping as usual to a decision which might change all his plans save that dealing with his destination.

But that was his way. Nothing was ever too much trouble for Wakefield Damon to do for a friend. He at once halted his preparations and rode back to Shopton with Tom and Mary, squeezed in between them on the narrow seat of the runabout, and interviewed the physicians that were attending Mr. Nestor.

What he learned about the chance Mr. Nestor had of surviving such a journey as was proposed satisfied Mr. Damon that he could take a chance with the invalid. When he went to the Nestor house and told the family in his blusterous way that he proposed bearing the sick man off with him, as a prisoner if need be, he scattered the gloom of that household most effectively.

"You are the dearest man who ever lived!" cried Mary, throwing herself into his arms.

"I'm going to tell Tom that," threatened Mr. Damon. "Bless my love-knots, but that is the greatest compliment I ever had."

Mary blushed, but her eyes shone upon him just the same. Mrs. Nestor was very grateful. The declaration made the most impression on the sick man.

"To Denmark and Iceland?" he said. "Places I have never seen! I shall like it. You give me a chance for life, I do believe, Brother Damon."

"Never mind the sugar-plums," replied Mr. Damon. "We've got to go in a hurry, for there is a certain steamship I want to take. Bless my seven-league boots! but we have got to do some tall traveling."

It was all over and the invalid had been carried off by the boisterous Wakefield Damon. Tom Swift stood with Mary and her mother on the porch of their house and watched the two taxicabs, with the travelers and the baggage, disappear toward the railroad station. Mr. Nestor would not hear to any of them following him to the train.

"I hope everything will be all right with him," sighed Mrs. Nestor.

"Well, everything will be all right with us here!" cried Mary, smiling at Tom. "We have Tom to look out for us."

"Ah, Tom is such a help," agreed the anxious woman. "But I hope Dr. Raddiker was right. It is a long way to Iceland, and the cold sea voyage may do him more harm than good."

CHAPTER IX

THE KEEL IS LAID

"You have convinced yourself that this amount will finance the great scheme, have you, Tom?" asked Ned Newton, leaning back in his chair in the private office of the Swift Construction Company at Shopton. "We can't be too particular about the financial end of it."

"All right, Old Cerberus," laughed Tom Swift, who called his friend everything from the "Watchdog of the Treasury" to "Tightwad, the Penny Squeezer." "I've told you how far I have gone. I have O.K.'d several contracts for parts of the *Winged Arrow*——"

"Is that going to be the name of the boat?"

"I think so. We have to call her something. I am going to lay her keel—the keel of her boat-cabin—within the fortnight, if circumstances permit. If I don't fall down on it, Ned, she is going to be a worthy craft!"

"Naturally," Ned rejoined loyally. "You would not waste your time on anything mediocre, I am sure."

"Many, many thanks," returned Tom, getting up to bow to his treasurer.

"But tell me more about it. Let's have the particulars," said Ned, with interest.

"I will give you a few figures to consider," Tom said promptly, picking up a paper from his desk and reading from it. "The boat will be sixty feet long. That is about the length of the keel. She will have cabin space for ten or twelve people. I plan to have the wings spread at least one hundred and ten feet. She will be driven by two Liberty motors, each of four hundred horsepower. If I can't get a hundred miles an hour speed out of her I shall be gravely disappointed."

"Whew! Some boat!" muttered Ned. "But if it is practical, we may make some money out of it."

"Miser!" chuckled Tom.

"That's all right. Just spending money for the fun of it will get you nowhere," said Ned soberly. "It is going to cost a pretty penny. But if you can sell it to the Government, for instance; or some government——"

"Whatever I build, is at the service of our country," Tom said promptly. "But I am not going to peddle my inventions to other nations. I don't need to."

"'Pride goeth before a fall,'" quoted Ned Newton. "The time may come when the Swift

Construction Company will need cash. Then
these experiments of yours will breed some
ducats."

"This flying boat is my pet project, Ned,"
Tom said soberly. "I believe a deal of experimenting is going on all over the world in the
constructing of seaplanes. It is the most practical end of the flying game."

"So it appears."

"Then, we want to keep in the lead. The Swift
Construction Company ought to put out a boat
that will lead them all, even if we never make a
penny out of it."

"Don't talk that way!" urged Ned. "Our
books have got to show a balance on the right
side at the end of the year. Go ahead. Do all
the experimenting you want. But in the end,
Tom Swift, I shall expect you to evolve something that will pay the company *big*."

In secret Tom believed that was exactly what
he should do. But he did not like to be too san-
guine. After all, a good many of the ideas he
had evolved regarding the new invention were
so embryonic that he hesitated to go into particulars about them with Ned, or even with his
father.

Barton Hopkins had been a dreamer, like his
son, in his younger days. But age usually makes
a man critical. Tom did not want anybody to

tell him a thing could not be done until he had
tried it out himself and was satisfied that it was
impossible.

During these days after the departure of Mr.
Damon and Mary's father for Denmark Tom
lived in a good deal of a mental haze. He allowed
nothing, at least, to interfere any more with his
consideration of the new invention. Rad Sampson declared that the younger Swift was so absorbed by his work that he did not know what
he ate half the time.

"Dat boy sartain sure work hisself sick,"
grumbled the old colored man. "Dem things he
is playin' wid take all his mind off'n 'portant
things. Suah do!"

To Rad the pleasures of the table were far
more important than the building of a flying boat
that was to astonish the world.

"Some shingles an' pigs' bladders and pieces
of string—huh!" grumbled Rad. "Let dis yere
Koku play wid 'em. They jest de sort ob things
childern and heathens plays wid. I's 'shamed of
Mars' Tom."

The model Tom had built upon his bedroom
table, however, was all that Rad saw of the flying
boat. It was merely a rough suggestion of what
the young inventor hoped the *Winged Arrow*
would be when it was done. In one of the locked
rooms attached to his office suite at the works

he was working out in full detail the mysterious seaplane.

The workmen, even the most trusted ones, had little idea as yet as to what Tom Swift was about. But when a part of the erecting shop was cleared for the keel of the big boat they all grew excited. The Swift Construction Company was about to evolve another wonder!

When Tom himself appeared in the erecting shop in working clothes the men might well be sure that something of importance was under way. There was another sign that never failed. Koku, the giant, was close at hand.

The strange fellow had believed for a long time now that his beloved young "Master" was threatened by malign enemies, both of a physical and spiritual kind. No talking to Koku or explanation of religious matters could convince the giant that there were not actual "devils," as well as evil influences, at work in the world.

Tom had been in so many perils from certain evil people who were opposed to the Government during the war, and who were the young inventor's personal enemies as well, that the poor savage expected harm to come to his master at any and all times.

When Tom was working around machinery or engaged in any matter where there were other men about—especially rough looking men—

Koku did not intend to be far away from Tom Swift. He watched the young fellow and all those who approached him with a gaze as sharp as that of a lynx.

Sometimes Tom turned around quickly to find the giant almost at his elbow, his savage gaze enough to startle any one. Koku's eyes had the quality of a cat's. They narrowed to a wicked slit in the daytime, and were yellow. At night they expanded and were glowing, and it had often been proved that he could see farther and more distinctly in the dark than any American of European descent.

As Tom moved about briskly, appointing each man his task, advising here and ordering there, Koku was sometimes quite put to it to keep within arm's reach of his master. But, at least, he never lost sight of him, and the giant could move so quickly and lightly that he was seldom in anybody's way.

Having selected most of his mechanics with much care and after giving heedful attention to their characters as well as to their ability as workmen, Tom had no suspicion at this time that a single man in the works felt any enmity toward him. He laughed with his father and with Ned Newton, therefore, over Koku's careful watch upon him and those about him.

And yet, there arose a situation, totally unexpected, almost inexplicable, which might have been considered with justice a direct attempt to injure the young inventor. And in the thrilling action of the moment in question it seemed that Tom Swift would neither carry through his attempt to build a wonderful flying boat nor accomplish any other future marvel.

Certain steel trusses were being arranged along the measured length of the floor of the shop devoted to the laying of the keel. The keel had reached Shopton in sections, and nobody outside the works could have guessed what the shining metal parts were as the trucks brought them from the railroad to the shops.

The traveling crane picked up these numbered parts of the keel and in succession delivered them to the gang handling the emplacement on the trusses. The prow was railroaded to the far end of the building and eased into place. The second section was brought forward.

The gang was busy with this while the crane, traveling upon an overhead rail, was supposed to drift down the length of the shop again, drawn by the power of the stationary engine. The crane and its swinging hooks and loops of chain traveled almost silently.

No workman around the keel noted that the crane stopped half way to the door of the shop. It seemed to have fouled, for it stopped abruptly

and the overhead rail shivered through its entire
length.

Tom had mounted to one of the trusses and
with voice and gesture was advising his helpers
how he wished the last piece of the keel placed.
The clanging of other machinery, the echo of
hammers, the roar of escaping steam, well nigh
deafened them all.

Of a sudden Koku, the giant, emitted a shriek
that might have been envied by a steam locomotive! He leaped directly at Tom. He hurdled
two of the trusses as though they were no higher
than croquet hoops, and with broad-spread arms
and clutching hands, lunged at the young inventor.

"Look out there, Mr. Tom!" cried one of the
men, making his voice heard even above Koku's
roar. "That giant's gone crazy!"

Before the young fellow could turn to see what
was threatening him, Koku was upon him and
had seized him in his mighty arms.

CHAPTER X

BAD LUCK

THE great leap of the excited giant carried him under and beyond the overhead rail from which the traveling crane hung. The wind of the rebounding crane seemed to sweep Koku and Tom aside. They escaped the swinging hooks and chains by a very close margin.

But all of the unobservant workmen were not so fortunate. Two of them were knocked senseless by the chain, one with a broken shoulder blade, the other with a cut on his head that bled profusely. Several others were knocked down.

Tom was up with a yell, wrenched himself from Koku's grasp, and started down the shop with the speed of a deer.

"Who did that? Stop your engine! Throw off the power!" he yelled.

But already the man in charge of the power governing the crane had come to his senses. He had thrown over the lever and shut off the power. The swinging loops of heavy steel links were now at the far end of the shop.

The accident was, for a time, seemingly inexplicable. The crane traveling toward the shop door had been seemingly stuck. The controller had been thrown twice to start it. And when the fouled crane had started, it had rushed backward instead of forward. Only Koku's sharp gaze had observed it, and his quick action had saved Tom Swift from disaster.

An ambulance was sent for to take the two more seriously injured men to the hospital. Meanwhile the general opinion in the erecting shop was that a deliberate attempt had been made against the young inventor's life.

Koku glared at everybody who came anywhere near his master. He marched up and down within a stride or two of Tom, and flexed his big muscles and muttered threats in his own tongue. The half civilized creature, who was usually the mildest person imaginable, had now become a figure to strike terror to the bravest.

Before anything further was done to the keel of the flying boat Tom made an exhaustive examination of the traveling crane, the cables attached to it, and the steel rail from which its truck hung. He trusted the engineman, who was an old employee. And he could not think of any man or boy about the erecting shop that wished the company—or himself—ill.

"It's a jinx, boss," declared one of the older

men. "Bad luck! And I have a feeling in my
bones that it's only the beginning."

"Come, Carney!" commanded Tom Swift.
"You take something to get rid of any such feeling. Don't talk that way and let the other men
hear you. Of course there is a perfectly reason-
able explanation of the accident."

"That doesn't stop it from being bad luck just
the same," muttered the man.

A thorough scrutiny of the line of the crane's
travel finally resulted in a single explanation of
the accident. Tom picked up a loop of steel cable—a piece perhaps two feet long when straight-
ened—which showed marks of the wheels of the
traveler.

"This loop must have been left hanging to the
rail by some careless repair man and, after that
last trip of the crane, it shifted and slid along
the rail to that spot where the machinery fouled,"
Tom declared.

"Now, somebody is at fault in this. It has
cost the Swift Construction a great deal of money
for employees' compensation, as well as the wage
loss for this breakdown. If I ever find out who
the careless man is, I'll fire him. Carelessness is
the most dangerous thing in the world. Our lives
are not safe when such a man is around. Now
let's see what more we can do about laying this
keel."

It did seem, however, as though the old machinist had somehow hit it right about the "jinx." Bad luck seemed to accompany the assembling of the body of the flying boat. Little accidents happened daily. Men were hurt, tools were broken, delays occurred. Tom got into a touchy state that even Ned Newton recognized.

"You'd better knock off on this flying boat and get a change of action," Ned advised. "Go somewhere with Mary and her mother. Take a rest."

"You'd better take a rest yourself," returned Tom sharply, but grinning. "I would fly all to pieces just now if I had to be idle. You know how it is with me, Ned. I have to work it off. And I can think or talk about nothing now but the *Winged Arrow.*"

"It looks to me," said the pessimistic Ned, "that that is one arrow that will never be shot. I have been looking it over, and all it seems to be is a great pontoon—as clumsy as can be."

"You are a cheerful beggar!" snapped Tom Swift. "What do you expect to see at this stage of the work, I'd like to know?"

"Well, two things I hate to see are the bills and the labor-cost account," grumbled Ned. "You are going to strain the credit of this company before you get through, Tom."

"It's lucky dad and I held onto so much of the stock," rejoined the young inventor, with a sudden grin. "We are the only two with vision. You are terribly sordid, Ned."

"I'm terribly practical," grumbled his friend. "Money is one of the hardest things to get hold of and the slipperiest things to hold on to in the world. I wish I could impress these facts on your mind."

"Say not so!" gibed Tom. "Them cruel words break me hear-r-r-t, Ned. Wait till you see the *Winged Arrow* take to the air from Lake Carlopa——"

"Wait till I do!" exclaimed Ned, and for once the friends were so far apart in their opinions that they almost quarreled.

Koku lurked about the shop day and night on the watch for somebody or something that tried to trouble his young master.

"Him evil one at work," the giant declared to Rad Sampson.

"Lawsy-marcy!" grumbled Rad, rolling his eyes. "Yo' suah has a close't acquaintance wid Ol' Satan, Koku. How'd yo' git dat way?"

A fire started among some oil-soaked waste behind the stationary engine in the erecting shop. A power belt stripped unexpectedly and balled up the machinery for most of one day. Certain castings were discovered to have faults in them that would have endangered the success of the flying boat if the faults had not been seen in time.

Altogether a less determined fellow than Tom Swift would possibly have been tempted to abandon his plans—at least, for the time being. But the young inventor was utterly given up to the building of the flying boat, and nothing but personal disaster would have stopped him.

The work did go on apace, after all. Tom's energy and ingenuity were sufficient for the accomplishment of a deal that might seem impossible to men much older than himself. As his plans developed for the flying boat, he worked harder and for longer hours. Mary declared that he even neglected her.

The young girl realized, however, that her father's illness had delayed Tom's beginning upon his new invention. Now he felt that he must work the harder to make up the lost time.

Mary and her mother were getting accustomed to the idea of Mr. Nestor's absence. Besides receiving a cheerful letter written by the invalid before he sailed from New York with Mr. Damon for Denmark, they had received two wireless messages sent while the travelers were at sea.

Then followed a considerable wait before the letter arrived from Denmark describing the voyage and explaining how they were to reach Iceland the following month. Mr. Nestor was much more cheerful and was feeling better already. He said that Mr. Damon was blessing everything in the universe because of their delays, but that they hoped to reach Iceland and the village of Rose-stone while the weather was still comparatively mild.

Of course Tom Swift was interested in all that Mary was interested in. Nevertheless he had pretty well put out of his mind any anxiety for the invalid. He believed that Mr. Nestor was in very capable hands, for the eccentricities of Wakefield Damon did not keep him from being a loyal friend and a jolly traveling companion.

As Mr. Barton Swift said, Tom ate, slept, and lived *flying boat!* Nothing else in the world seemed just then of so much importance as the building of the *Winged Arrow,* which was the name Tom had selected for the seaplane.

"If the craft accomplished the speed Tom expects, she will be well named," the elder Swift said in confidence to Ned Newton.

Secretly Ned was quite as proud of his chum's ability and brains as was Tom's father. But he felt it his duty to put brakes on whenever he saw a great amount of money being risked in an enterprise that might be a fizzle in the end.

To Tom's mind the weeks passed with astonishing celerity. Mary was looking for news from Iceland when the huge flying boat was removed in sections from the erecting shop and trundled down to the edge of Lake Carlopa on trucks.

There it was once more put together on the ways, every part tested for faults, the motors put aboard and connected with the propellers, and then, like any ship, she was launched into the water. It was a gala day in Shopton when the marvel was given her first bath. The works closed down and everybody connected with the Swift Construction Company was on hand to see the launching.

Mary Nestor broke the bottle of grape juice on the nose of the *Winged Arrow* as she struck the water and was splashed in return by the water as the plane "made a hole" in the lake.

It was a rough and windy day when this took place; but the boat merely rocked gently upon the surface after that first splash. It made a very brave appearance indeed.

"Mebbe the jinx is finished," said Carney, the old workman, in confidence when the launching was over. "Anyway, we got the thing out of the shops without killing anybody. And that's a good thing."

Tom Swift was not thinking about Carney's "jinx" on this day. He was much too deeply absorbed in the fact of the boat's being in the water. Then, too, he had a small puzzle in his mind while the ceremony of launching was taking place.

In the crowd of spectators was a man whose

face he knew. The man watched proceedings with an exceedingly keen scrutiny. His interest in the huge flying boat was professional, Tom was sure. He began to have some uneasiness about the man, for, although he was sure he had seen him before, Tom Swift could not remember where he had seen him or what his name was.

CHAPTER XI

THE TRIAL

Ned Newton took dinner at the Swift house that evening, and in the course of the meal he asked Tom:

"Did you chance to see a man in a frock coat, a gardenia in his buttonhole, and wearing a top hat at the lake to-day? Little peaked black mustache and a whisp of goatee? Rather Frenchy looking."

"He is just the chap I have been worrying about!" exclaimed the young inventor.

"Why worry about him?" demanded Ned, while even Mr. Swift looked at his son in some surprise.

"Because it worries me to know that I've seen a man but am unable to place him. Do you have any idea, Ned, who he is?"

"That is what I was asking you—or attempting to," returned Ned.

"He knows seaplanes, at least," observed Tom. "I must have seen him—or his picture, perhaps."

"He was a complete stranger to me," declared Ned.

"His face is familiar to me. And I am a bit scary of him," confessed Tom. "He looked the new boat over as though he understood everything about her. Humph! There are some unpatented parts that I would not care to have stolen."

"The man could scarcely steal them *in his eye,*" remarked Mr. Swift.

"I am not so sure of that. But it may be that because of trouble we have had in the past, I am suspicious with little cause."

"You have caught that from Koku," laughed Ned Newton.

"Maybe the boy is more than half right," rejoined Tom, referring to the giant. "Carney, in the shops, has said he 'had a feeling in his bones' that there was a 'jinx' on the boat. Humph! I have to say I don't believe in such things——"

"Whether you do believe in evil spirits or not?" interposed Ned.

"Well, that may be so. After all, admitting the existence of bad luck is to encourage it, they say. But that has nothing much to do with the dapper little man with the spike mustache and goatee and the flower in his buttonhole. He was spick and span——"

"Like most Frenchmen? That is one reason

why I almost always like the French," declared
Ned.

"I'd just like to know who he is," repeated
Tom. "Anyway, I am going to ask you, Ned,
to increase the special guards about the cove over
there where the plane rests. I am not yet ready
to give other people the benefit of my discoveries."

"So Koku is not guard enough?" chuckled
Ned Newton.

"He has to sleep once in a while. Besides, a
well dressed man awes Koku a whole lot," and
Tom smiled. "And this chap you speak of could
put it all over the innocent savage."

They decided to have a special number of
guards who should remain at the cove where the
launching had taken place, at least, until the time
of the try-out. And Tom and his men strained
every effort to complete the flying boat and send
it into the air as quickly as possible.

Tom kept three shifts a day at work. But
only the most skilled of his men could be trusted
on the job, so the crews were small. However,
there was not an hour of the twenty-four save
from Saturday evening until Monday morning
when the hammers did not ring or the steam
drills puff or the riveters clatter on the *Winged
Arrow*.

That shore of Lake Carlopa became a very

popular resort for sightseers during the ensuing fortnight. The newspapers had got hold of the idea that Tom Swift was about to reveal to the world another marvel, and the reporters would have annoyed the young inventor a good deal had it not been for Ned Newton.

Ned believed in a certain amount of publicity, and the stories he furnished the newspaper reporters, if not particularly scientific, were at least interesting. Tom Swift's new flying boat was a first page leader for several days before the test day.

Tom was watchful for the reappearance of the man whose presence at the launching had disturbed him; but the French looking person did not again come to the cove. At least, Tom did not see the stranger. And as the hour approached when the *Winged Arrow* would be ready for her trial flight the young inventor gradually forgot all outside matters. He did not even go to the Nestor house to learn if the invalid and Mr. Damon had been heard from again. He began to sleep aboard the flying boat, as the cabin was practically finished.

This central portion of the pontoon, or boat, was arranged so as to utilize every inch of space. There were folding berths for eight. The cabin could be divided by a curtain if passengers of opposite sexes were included in any party. Meals

for officers and passengers would be served here,
too, the galley being directly aft.

In contradistinction to the ordinary sailing
craft, the quarters of the crew of the *Winged
Arrow* were in her tail, or after-part. These ma-
chinists would be furnished hammocks to sleep
in. The prow of the boat, where the mechanism
of the powerful searchlights was housed, was
built of well-leaded glass so that an unobstructed
view ahead and above, as well as below and on
either side, could be obtained.

As the huge machine floated on the water of
the lake cove, it seemed very awkward and as
though it would be unmanageable. The opinions
of sightseers who came to stare were as amus-
ing as they were often silly. It seemed to be the
consensus of these opinions that Tom Swift
never intended to try to fly the huge boat, but
that it was merely a "stock jobbing" scheme. It
was told that stock in the Swift Construction
Company was being sold at fabulous prices on
the strength of this flying boat that was doomed
to failure.

"Gee!" ejaculated Ned Newton, hearing this,
"I wish it was as easy to sell shares in a bona
fide invention as these people seem to think it is
in a fake. Money would be easy enough to
raise."

It was true that a fortune—and not a small

fortune—had been expended upon the building of the *Winged Arrow*. The treasurer of the Swift Construction Company might well be anxious.

"If she's a fizzle, Tom, my boy," he said mournfully, "we'll all have to go into bankruptcy."

"She may not be an unqualified success right at the start," rejoined the young inventor, with confidence. "But I mean to make her fly and sail and make a proper landing on the earth and water before I am through."

The morning of the day on which the test flight of the new plane was to occur, Tom Swift was awakened at eight o'clock, a late hour for him, by the ringing of his private radio-telephone. He rolled over in bed and grabbed the instrument, removed the receiver and sleepily shouted:

"Hullo!"

"Tom Swift?" came the voice over the wire— a voice that was quite unfamiliar to the inventor.

"Speaking," replied Tom, yawning. "Excuse me. Who is it?"

"That does not matter—just now," said the voice clearly. "I want you to do me a favor."

"What is that?"

"I understand you mean to try out your new seaplane to-day?"

"That is a private matter," returned Tom, awakened now to full caution.

"Agreed. But I would like the chance of going with you on the try-out."

"What's that?" demanded Tom, in amazement. "You want to join my mechanics and myself on what may be a dangerous voyage?"

"Exactly. I am interested in your invention. I may be more interested when I see personally how it works. And if that is so——"

"Well, sir?" shot in Tom, not at all pleased.

"If the plane acts as you seem to think it will, I may be able to finance your building several of the machines and under circumstances that will make it well worth your while to sign a contract."

Tom got a grip on himself almost at once. He replied in a most casual way:

"I am not at all sure that you could interest me in any such proposition, even if I knew who you were and was assured of your good intent. In the first place, this is an entirely private venture, and I have no thought of selling the plane, or any like it. It may be some time before I consider the machine perfect. In any case, I do not know you——"

"Tell me that I am to be one of your sailing party and I will present my credentials," interrupted the strange voice quickly.

Naturally Tom Swift had thought, as soon as he was fully awakened, of the dapper man whose presence at the launching of the *Winged Arrow* had puzzled both Ned Newton and himself. Although the man had the appearance of a foreigner, this voice betrayed not the least accent. The English used seemed meticulously correct, which is, however, a mark sometimes of the speech of well educated foreigners.

"I can make no arrangements over the telephone," Tom said bluntly. "Especially with people of whose identity I know nothing. In addition, in the present case, and regarding your request, I must refuse absolutely. Nobody goes with me on the test trip save chosen workmen and Mr. Newton. I must distinctly say No!" concluded Tom.

"If ready cash would be an object?" began the voice again, but Tom said once more: "No, sir!" and closed the receiver.

But all the time he was bathing and dressing, and even while he was eating Rad Sampson's cakes and chops, the young inventor puzzled his brain over the incident and the possible identity of the person who had awakened him.

"He is keeping mighty close tabs on me, whoever he is," thought Tom. "Even knew I had this radio-telephone installed on the boat. And he must represent somebody with plenty of money. Humph, I wonder what the game really is!

"Business rivals, I presume. And yet, that's queer, too. I know no one who's in desperate need of my ideas and plans just now. Humph! queer's no word for it."

As he said, he had already selected his crew for the first flight of the *Winged Arrow*. The men were volunteers, of course, and they had signed off their personal indemnity before he accepted them.

It was true, Ned Newton was to accompany him. Ned was almost as able to pilot the boat as Tom himself. Mr. Swift merely came down to the lake to bid them good-bye and watch the flight of the craft. He helped and advised Tom, but he left the active work wholly in his son's capable hands now.

The crowd that gathered numbered several hundred Shopton folk and probably some strangers. But as the preparations for the test were concluded Tom scrutinized the groups of spectators sharply for a sight of the man who had previously interested him.

Whether it was that individual who had got in communication with Tom early that morning or not, the young inventor did not see him in the crowd.

"Did you see him?" he asked Ned Newton, as

the treasurer of the company came aboard at the last moment.

"See who?" demanded Ned, in some surprise.

"The Frenchman, as you called him."

"No, I had forgotten all about him."

"I have an idea that he has not forgotten about us—or about the *Winged Arrow*," Tom said reflectively.

CHAPTER XII

IN PERIL

THERE was a deal of running about by the crew, getting ready for the flight. Ned Newton stared at his friend, the inventor, and asked softly:

"Just what are you getting at, Tom? Do you think that stranger is around again?"

"I am pretty sure of it," said Tom, in the same low tone. He swiftly related what he had heard by radio-telephone that morning. "The thing is mysterious, to say the least."

"I'll say so!" agreed Ned, wagging his head. "I don't see what it can mean."

"We will hear more of it," said Tom with confidence. "But probably not to-day. At any rate, no stranger goes on the *Winged Arrow* this first trip."

Although Rad Sampson had got breakfast for his beloved young master in the galley of the seaplane that morning, he got off in a hurry when the time approached for the trial flight.

"I been up in de air befo', big man," he said to Koku. "But, belieb me! I ain't hankering to go up no mo' till Gabriel blows his trump. No-suh!"

"Who Gab'el?" demanded the giant. "What he blow for?"

"Ma goodness! Of all de ignerances I ever heard tell of!" groaned Rad. "I don't see how you is ever gwine to git past Saint Peter, Koku."

Koku merely blinked. He was worried about Tom's going up in the plane without him. But nothing much else disturbed his simple mind just then.

Tom tried out the motors several times. The propellers worked perfectly. The hawsers holding the plane to the dock were thrown off, and then the big airship began to move. Tom headed her out into the lake.

The crowd ashore cheered wildly as the nose of the great seaplane rose from the surface. She was then surrounded by a cloud of spray and her motors were roaring. She lifted more and more, and soon those ashore could see beneath the entire length of the boat's keel.

She hung above the water for a time, swerving in a quarter circle so as to head inshore again. Her wide wings and the two wheels underneath for land travel made the machine look like some huge winged insect or an antediluvian bird.

The plane soared higher and higher, spiraling upward over the heads of the interested spectators. From the ground it seemed as though no such huge machine could be floated in the air. It must come crashing down to earth again!

But still it mounted. Mr. Barton Swift, with binoculars at his eyes, watched the ascent with keen interest and some apprehension. He saw its wavering course, and realized that the balance of the huge plane was not at all perfect.

Smaller and smaller grew the plane to the naked eye. That it wabbled in its course meant little to any of the spectators save the old inventor. He knew that the crew of the *Winged Arrow* was in trouble, if not in danger!

Suddenly the old gentleman was aware of the presence beside him of a man who likewise followed the course of the careening plane through binoculars. Mr. Swift cast a sharp glance upon this individual.

He was very well dressed in a spick and span afternoon costume and wore a flower in his buttonhole. His dab of black mustache and goatee almost seemed painted upon his pale face. He brought the glasses down from his eyes and looked at Mr. Barton Swift.

"What do you say, sir?" he asked. "Is she not making a heavy passage?"

Mr. Swift was instantly cautious. Tom had

not spoken to his father about this mysterious individual. But the old inventor had experienced so much interference on his own part from rivals, and had observed what Tom had sometimes suffered as well, that he was not likely to divulge his own private opinion to this stranger.

"You understand," he said quietly, "that no flying machine shoots into the sky like an arrow, even if it is named *Arrow.*"

"True, true," said the other eagerly. "It is a good point, sir. But there! You see?" He pointed again eagerly with his cane. "Did you see her roll then?"

"An air-pocket, most likely," Mr. Swift said calmly.

But he knew that the *Winged Arrow* was not yet high enough to find those atmospheric "holes" which sometimes turn a plane over and often cause wreck and disaster. Unlike the smaller flying machines, the seaplane was not likely to take a tail-spin and come down, unmanageable, in that way. But she might buckle and break her back in one of those aerial vacuums.

"Is it your opinion, Mr. Swift," asked the stranger in his too perfect English, "that this plane will be a success?"

"My son evidently believes so, and that is enough for me," returned the old gentleman. "I am no longer active in our business. I could not give a professional opinion upon the matter at this time."

"Ah! You are cautious!" exclaimed the stranger.

"I am careful as to whom I talk with—yes," admitted Mr. Swift pointedly. "Come, sir! you have as good eyesight as I have. Arrive at your own judgments."

He turned away from the stranger then and gazed only at the rising plane. But even he had small idea of what was going on aboard the *Winged Arrow* at just this time.

Tom Swift and Ned Newton were in the bow of the seaplane when she swam out of the cove. The steering gear, as well as the tubes to the mechanician's compartment, were right at Tom's hand. Besides, the speed and altitude indicators were here. Like every other plane, the *Winged Arrow* was a "one-mind" machine. A single individual must govern it all.

But, as Tom had long since pointed out, in testing flying machines of all sizes, for safety's sake, there should be a second man in the cockpit of even a monoplane. In handling this huge plane it would be a reckless thing for only one man to be at the steering and other gear. A second must always be at hand to jump in and take charge if anything happened to the chief steersman, or pilot.

Therefore Tom had trained Ned Newton for just this emergency. Ned had learned with the inventor himself as the *Winged Arrow* was building how to handle the gears which controlled all the movements of the plane. He could start, stop, raise, lower, and otherwise control the huge machine about as well as Tom himself.

But on this maiden trip Tom allowed nobody save himself to touch the mechanism in the bow of the boat.

When the craft had gained speed enough on the surface of the lake Tom lifted her nose cautiously and, in a minute, sent her sliding skyward. The slant of her nose became more abrupt after a few minutes, and Tom shifted the levers so that the flying boat aimed shoreward once again.

At that time she was sailing not many yards above the lake. As she came inshore the pilot began to make her spiral upward. At first her motion was merely a rocking one and not at all unpleasant to the crew distributed about the boat.

Suddenly, as the plane rose at a sharper slant, she began to roll. Ned shouted to ask his chum what had happened, for the windows were open on the sides of the prow and the drumming of the wings and the rush of the air engendered a noise that was almost deafening.

"I don't know," admitted Tom, shaking his head. "Remember, this is my first trip in the thing as well as yours. Why should *I* be supposed to know all about it?" and he grinned cheerfully as he looked at his chum.

But in a moment the car took another roll. Ned thought it was about to turn turtle. It was no laughing matter.

"Did you make her so she would fly just as well upside down as on even keel?" he demanded, having closed the windows.

Tom looked serious. His hand was on the steering levers, or controls. He knew that this rolling motion must wrench the framework of the plane enormously. They heard the beams groan, and somewhere a cable snapped.

"Listen to that, will you?" exclaimed Ned.

The plane kept on even keel for a few moments longer. They had been in peril, as Tom well knew. Were they now safe?

He lifted the nose of the craft a bit more and again the wings dipped sideways and the boat rolled "upon her beam ends," as would have been said of a seagoing craft.

"Stop her, Tom! Stop her!" shouted Ned, scrambling up from the floor, where he had fallen when the craft rolled.

But Tom knew that to shut off power and

"stop" the flying boat would court greater disaster.

For some unknown reason the craft had lost her balance, and when she rolled over the other way it seemed to the young inventor as though she must go completely over, her wings be wrenched away, and the great craft fall to the earth in a tremendous crash!

CHAPTER XIII

A SECOND TEST

AFTER his second shout of alarm, Ned Newton remained quiet. After all, he did not lack either physical or moral courage. He had not entered into this test of the flying boat without knowing very well that something might go wrong and that a fatal disaster for all was possible.

How the mechanicians were affected, the inventor and Ned did not know just then. The members of the crew in the tail of the boat made no comment through the speaking tube. As for comments by anybody on the earth that might be watching the careening plane, Tom Swift had made no provision for receiving such a communication. There was radio on board the *Winged Arrow,* but it was not in use during this test.

Nor could any advice, even from Mr. Barton Swift, have aided the young inventor in this serious emergency. Something was wrong with the balance of the seaplane. Just what it was, Tom had not yet the first idea. He was as much puzzled as anybody else could have been.

The rolling of the huge structure continued. Had it not been put together with such care, the plane would never have withstood the second roll.

Ned, who had gained his feet and who clung to one of the hand-rails with which the compartment in the nose of the boat was furnished, now was silent. He watched his chum's movements with great anxiety, but he did not interfere by either speech or act with Tom's attempts to govern the craft.

The inventor watched the needles of the several indicators connected with the mechanism of the plane. Some of these gyrated crazily when the boat rolled. But there was an arrow on one dial that stood still.

This dial had nothing to do with the driving of the plane. At first it did not enter Tom Swift's mind that this dial—or what it registered—was at all important to the flight of the seaplane.

It was the indicator which registered the amount of compressed air that filled the "skin" of the boat. This hollow between the outer and inner hull of the craft had to do with the balance and security of the plane when she had to be brought down into the sea in rough weather.

Tom's experiments with the pigs' bladders and the hollow bamboo had resulted in an attempt to overcome boisterous waves through the weight of compressed air between the two skins of the boat's hull. How it was going to work when the *Winged Arrow* chanced to descend upon a rough sea, was yet to be proved.

He noted the unwavering needle on this particular indicator several times while the plane was rolling without getting from it any inspiration at all. Then, suddenly, he uttered a mighty shout, grabbed for the flexible speaking tube, and yelled to his chief mechanician:

"Brannigan! Start the pump! Get busy!"

"What pump, boss?" was the surprised query from the tail of the boat.

"Compressed air! Isn't but one, Brannigan! Fill the skin!"

"All right, boss! Are you goin' down?"

"Not if I can help it. I want to stay up," answered Tom, and dropped the tube.

"What's the idea?" demanded Ned, staring at him.

"I don't quite know what the idea is myself, yet," confessed the young inventor. "But something has got to be done, and I am willing to try— Here we go again!"

Once more the huge, groaning structure rolled. If it looked bad to those on the ground, consider how the crew of the *Winged Arrow* felt!

The usual kind of an equilibrator—that used in the government of most dirigible balloons and other flying craft—was a part of the *Winged*

Arrow's equipment, but in this strange case the instrument seemed to have no value at all. The great hull of the seaplane certainly did not balance.

Whether Tom drove the mechanism fast or slow, the rolling continued. No matter how strongly the structure was built, such wrenching must of necessity in time wreck the seaplane.

They were now a mile or more high in the air. If the plane fell apart at this altitude there would not be the smallest hope of escape for any of her crew. Tom had tried to descend, but she seemed to roll worse on a downward than on an upward slant.

"Brannigan! Make use of that pump!" Tom shouted through the tube.

"Aye, aye, sir!" came back the reply.

The finger on the dial had begun to move. The vacuum between the jackets of the hull began to fill with air. The plane regained an even keel again for a moment and Tom felt a tremor of the hull which he knew to be from the pressure of the air driven into the vacuum.

"What are you doing, Tom?" demanded Ned, putting his lips close to his friend's ear.

"Trying a new one. Great Scott! Ned, if my suspicion is right, I have worked a scheme for balancing an object floating in air which as far as I know is an entirely new trick. I have invented something—perhaps—without the first idea that I was doing anything extraordinary."

"Don't care what it is," replied Ned. "But if it is what is stopping the boat from rolling——"

"I believe it is! It is a new equilibrator! I believe it is going to work!"

"We're sitting pretty now," confessed Ned. "Don't try any more tricks till we are down again."

"Don't fret." Tom turned and spoke to Brannigan through the tube again. "Shut off! All right. Look out for yourselves back there. I am going to zoom."

The *Winged Arrow,* once more on even keel, began to descend in a great spiral. Closer and closer she came to the earth. There was Lake Carlopa and the cove from which she had taken to the air. After a time the two friends in the bow of the plane could see the spectators on the shore.

Tom Swift had quite recovered from his disturbance of mind. He believed he had by chance discovered something that really was of great value in the management of this type of seaplane. He wanted to talk it over with his father and make other experiments before being sure that he had guessed right.

After all, experiments in natural science are the chief paths to invention. Tom thought that he might have hit upon one of those lucky discoveries that often aid in the establishment of worthwhile knowledge.

When the seaplane finally took the water, the air chamber had to be relieved of pressure before the hull floated at a proper depth. Mr. Barton Swift noted this at once and turned to see if the well dressed and talkative stranger had taken note of this fact.

The man had disappeared. A motor-car shooting away along the road to Shopton suggested the manner in which the stranger might have gone. It was plain that for some reason the man did not wish to meet the younger Swift at this time.

Tom's father was so much interested in his son's discovery regarding the compressed air chamber and its value as an equilibrator that he forgot to speak of the stranger and his evident interest in the new flying boat.

Indeed, all those closely connected with Tom's experiments and with the success of the *Winged Arrow*, thought of little else for the next few days but the recurrent flights of the plane.

Tom took the jump-off from the surface of the lake and from the ground. They made successful landings on both the water and the earth. After each flight there were adjustments to make and changes in the mechanism. Tom and his crew worked day and night upon the wonderful flying boat.

At length Tom Swift was ready to make a longer flight in the winged boat. Until he had driven the *Winged Arrow* for a considerable distance without descending and until he had made a successful landing in rough water and a good jump-off from the same, the young inventor would not be satisfied that he had accomplished what he had set out to do.

He and Ned had forgotten the stranger who they believed had shown more than ordinary interest in the success or failure of the flying boat. And Mr. Swift had never mentioned that person to his son.

Indeed, so deeply engaged was Tom Swift in his new seaplane that other interests literally faded out of his mind. Before the flight to the ocean which he had determined on, however, Tom spent an evening with Mary Nestor and her mother.

At first Mrs. Nestor had heard so frequently from the invalid on his northern trip that she had lost much of her anxiety regarding Mr. Nestor's health and safety. But after the steamship had landed him and Mr. Damon at Reykjavik and Mr. Nestor had written one letter, his family had not heard a word from him.

"They were going into the interior—to Rosestone—the day following his letter," Mary explained to Tom. "What could have become of them after that we cannot imagine. Mother is becoming much worried again."

"You don't suppose that Iceland has postal communication as frequently as we have it here in the States, do you?" asked Tom. "It is sort of a barren land, I understand. They are all right. You'll get a letter any day now."

"It has been a month," Mrs. Nestor declared, shaking her head.

Tom laughed cheerfully. "No use talking. I see I'll have to provision this new plane of mine and take a trip in her to Iceland to look up that party."

"You could not go so far in the *Winged Arrow,* could you, Tom?" asked Mary.

"I do not know why not. That is exactly what I built her for—long trips. She is able to carry provisions for a party of ten and enough gasoline to last for at least a flight of two thousand miles."

"Two thousand miles without coming down?" cried Mary.

"About coming down, I don't know. I expect her to clear a hundred miles an hour when put to it. Even if we don't drive her more than fifty miles an hour, we could make a journey two thousand miles long in a little over a day and a half.

"And if she proves sea-worthy—if we **can**

bring her down and launch her into the air again from the surface of the ocean as easily as we do from Lake Carlopa—I would not be afraid of taking a trip to Iceland."

"Well, I just guess you won't!" cried Mary. "That would be very perilous, Tom. Even if father and Mr. Damon were in trouble up there, you could scarcely help them by flying to them in a seaplane."

Tom laughed too. The idea was odd enough. The use to which he expected to put the *Winged Arrow* was entirely practical.

That next morning they made the trial trip to the Atlantic. This test of the flying boat would be a real test. If she had to be brought down, either on land or sea, they would not be near head-quarters and the mechanicians aboard the plane must be equal to all repairs that might be neces-sary.

CHAPTER XIV

AMAZING NEWS

Tom Swift drove the *Winged Arrow* to a high altitude when she left Lake Carlopa on her first long voyage. It was a windy day, but pleasant. The weather indications were favorable for the journey, but the report from out at sea was that a storm had shaken up the shipping a good deal.

"We have that matter of balance and safety when taking to the water to settle, whatever else we may do," the inventor said to Ned Newton, who was again his companion. "The hollow sheath of the boat has proved a good thing while we are in the air; but I should hate to learn that I had planned something that turned out to be no good for the object I had in mind, even if it was useful in other ways."

Besides the two chums aboard the flying boat there were eight in the crew and a young man named Kingston who was a wireless operator. The *Winged Arrow* was supplied with the very latest instruments for wireless and radiophone operation, and Kingston was well trained in his business. He was, as well, a pleasant addition to the plane's company.

They flew so high that landmarks had to be scrutinized through the glasses to make sure of their nature. They passed over three states in reaching the coast. From their height it seemed as though the ocean were a hazy blue sheet of glass with a white or yellow line marking the shore. They scaled down nearer to it and saw great ships tossing on mighty billows and the surf viciously beating the sands of Cape Cod.

"Ho!" cried Ned. "I hope you are satisfied, Tom. It looks just as safe to land down there as though the ocean were a boiling cauldron."

"It is exactly what we have come to experience," declared Tom.

"Well, I hope everything is all right," grumbled his friend. "But I want to tell you right now that I would rather be on dry land than on this plane when she hits that sea. Whew!"

If Tom Swift felt any such fear he did not express it. But his face was rather grim as he scaled down the airways and brought the huge flying boat hovering above the tossing waves. To Brannigan, in the tail of the craft, he said:

"Test out your levers. See that everything is buzzing right. We are going to subject her to a severe test. All ready?"

"Aye, aye, sir!" rejoined Brannigan through the tube. "Let her go!"

Kingston, whose little coop was directly behind the pilot room, stuck his head out of his door at that moment and shouted:

"Have a care about bumping His Majesty's liner, *Cantoria*. She's right over yonder—you can see her. I just picked up a 'gram from her operator objecting to such big planes as ours being tried out in the steamship lanes."

"What's the matter with that limey?" demanded Ned. "Does he think he owns the whole ocean?"

"He is complaining to the U. S. Weather Bureau about us, just the same," declared the operator.

Tom shifted certain levers and the huge plane dived for the riotous surface of the sea. She swooped like a sea-eagle, skimmed the froth-capped waves for some distance, and then settled upon the water like a duck.

Foam and spray dashed completely over the wings and the boat's upperworks. They could scarcely see through the side ports. The roar of the waters pouring over the half buried craft was deafening. For the next few minutes the *Winged Arrow* was put through a test that surely would have wrecked a less strongly built craft.

The compressed air between the skins of the boat had to be increased considerably before she stopped rolling. The airtight pontoons at either end of the wings were not sufficient stabilizers. It seemed that Tom Swift's ingenuity had actually overcome a drawback that had baffled inventors of similar planes.

The flying boat floated like a well ballasted sailing craft. She climbed the steep waves, pitched over their tops, and slid to the depths of the trough between them with surprising ease. When the waves broke against her wings, leaping hungrily to overwhelm them, the perfect balance of the hull brought the whole ship back to an even keel in a few seconds.

Ned Newton was delighted. Aside from feeling some little disturbance in his stomach because of the boisterousness of the waves, he considered the test a great success.

"If this was my flying boat I certainly would slap myself on the back and give three cheers," he declared.

"You must be a remarkable contortionist to be able to do that," rejoined Tom, chuckling. "But I really am not posing. It seems as though we had hit the right idea. Hullo! What is the matter with Kingston?"

Through the glass half of the door to the radio coop they both saw that the operator seemed excited. He had the eartabs clamped to his head and was evidently listening in on something very important. With his right hand he wrote a few words quickly and then wheeled and beckoned Ned.

"Get this to the chief," he said abruptly. "It is relayed from Block Island. There may be more of it."

Ned wheeled about and thrust the paper into Tom's hand. The latter read the message at a glance:

"T. Swift, com. seaplane *Winged Arrow*, offshore, N. Atlantic, relay: Return immediately very important news of Damon and Nestor.— B. Swift."

Tom stared from the message to his friend.

"What do you know about that?" he exclaimed.

"Don't even know what it's all about," grumbled the treasurer of the Swift Construction Company.

"Look at it!" ejaculated Tom, and handed Ned the radio message.

"Great whales and little fishes!" gasped Ned, when he had read it. "It is from your father!"

"That's right."

"It can't be any joke, then," considered Ned. "Mr. Damon and Mary's father must be in trouble."

"But if they are up in Iceland and we are down here, what can I do to help them out of trouble?" cried Tom anxiously.

"That seems to be the question before the house," replied Ned. "Guess we'll have to go back home to find out. Your father is not very explicit, that is certain."

"He would not send this message at such a time unless the matter was urgent. I am glad we have been able to try out the *Winged Arrow* as well as we have. Poor Mr. Nestor! Suppose he has died up there? Or maybe Mr. Damon is ill."

"I hope not!" cried Ned.

"If it is anything like that, somebody will have to take passage at once for Iceland," Tom went on, in a worried way. "Mary and her mother have nobody to look to for help but father and me. Mary's uncle is traveling around the world, you know."

"Then the duty devolves on you, does it?" demanded the other young fellow. "And how about business? What about the Swift Construction Company? You will have to drop this flying boat right where she is!"

"I hope not," returned Tom, and he smiled again, though rather ruefully. "If we dropped her where she is, she would go to the bottom of a very deep part of the Atlantic, Ned."

"Don't joke! This is too serious," said his chum.

"You are right. It must be serious—particularly for the Nestors. If we have to delay the exploitation of the *Winged Arrow,* all right. The need of Mary and her mother comes first."

It might have been difficult to convince Ned of this; but he made no further rejoinder. It did seem too bad that, just as success seemed to have crowned Tom Swift's efforts in the building of a wonderful flying boat, a chance like this news from Iceland happened to postpone the final speed and other trials of the new invention.

Tom did not waste time even in replying to the wireless message. As they could not communicate direct with the plant at Shopton he knew that, barring accidents, the flying boat would make her landing behind the Swift Construction Company stockade before a radiogram could be delivered to his father.

Out of the boisterous sea the great flying boat rose like some huge waterfowl taking to the air. Her compressed air compartments were gradually emptied until she gained a perfect poise in the air, some mile or more above the sea.

Tom guided her in a half circle and she headed for the shore. The seaplane flew directly over the British ship, *Cantoria,* the captain of which had complained of the danger to ordinary shipping by the nearness of the plane.

"This fact will undoubtedly make the commander of that ship write to the *Times* when he gets back to London," chuckled Ned.

The seaplane rose higher as she neared the shore. The yellow streak of Cape Cod was only to be dimly distinguished through the lower windows of the pilot room. Night had fallen when the *Winged Arrow* spiraled over Shopton and the works. Tom made a ground landing instead of sinking to the surface of Lake Carlopa. He was in a hurry to get home.

The searchlights in the yard of the shops served as lighthouses for the plane's landing. She came down perfectly, bumping along the ground easily upon the wheels, and finally stopped not far from the highroad.

The Swift house was not far away. Aside from Koku, who had been on watch continually since the plane had flown away, there were few people to greet the crew. Tom and Ned left the mechanicians to attend to the flying boat and hurried up to the house.

Mr. Barton Swift, very much disturbed for him, was walking the library floor. He hurried to greet Tom and Ned, waving a blue cablegram in his hand.

"What is it, father?" Tom asked. "What has happened to Mr. Damon and Mary's father?"

"I don't know," confessed Barton Swift. "I have been wondering and worrying all the afternoon. And now I know less about it than I did at first."

"How is that?"

"It has crossed my mind that the message may be a fake. It may come from some schemer who wishes us ill. But on the face of it—here! Read it!"

He thrust the cablegram into Tom's hand. The young inventor read, and read it aloud for Ned Newton's benefit:

"Mes. Damon and Nestor lost with treasure chest on iceberg in Greenland Sea between Greenland and Iceland. *Kalrye* a wreck and our boats separated. Believe castaways alive on giant iceberg. Cable funds for rescue, or advise—Olaf Karofsen, com. *Kalrye*, Reykjavik."

CHAPTER XV

ON THE WINGS OF THE WIND

NED declared the message was a fake. He would not believe such an extraordinary tale could be true.

"Somebody wants to get you off the *Winged Arrow*," he said. "That fellow who hung around here at the launching—remember? The chap with the Frenchy look. I bet he represented some inventor who is trying to put out a machine like yours. This is a scheme to take your mind off your work and delay you."

"It can't delay me much now," said Tom, puzzled. "The flying boat has been proved practical—and is practically complete."

"I fear that something really terrible has happened to our friends up there in the Arctic," Mr. Swift broke in.

"The chief thing to do is to find out about it," Tom said vigorously. "We'll test this thing out—find out who Captain Olaf Karofsen of the *Kalrye* is."

"How are you going to do that and him in

Iceland?" scoffed Ned. "It will take you two
months or longer to get there."

"We have got to look into it and try to find
Mr. Damon and Mary's father, if it takes two
years," declared Tom.

He set to work at once with telephone and tel-
egraph and got information from everybody he
could think of regarding Iceland and its chief
seaport. He reached a representative of Icelandic
commercial interests at his home in Boston and
was told how to cable in the most direct way to
Reykjavik. The Merchants' Association there
verified Olaf Karofsen's statement of the wreck
of his motor schooner in the ice and the loss of
several passengers and their possessions.

Before morning Tom had a pretty complete
story of the disaster. It seemed that because of
the lateness of the season no steamship would sail
from Reykjavik at once, and Mr. Damon had
engaged the motor schooner, *Kalrye,* to take his
party over to a Greenland port from which a
fishing steamer would sail south before winter
really set in.

In the night and fog the *Kalrye* smashed into
a shelf of ice just below the surface, which
seemed to be part of a gigantic iceberg, the peaks
of which stood up out of the sea several miles
distant. Mr. Damon was known to carry with
him a chest of treasure which he had come to

Iceland to secure. With this chest Mr. Damon and his friend, with five sailors, had taken to one of the *Kalrye's* two boats. A heavy sea had smashed it against the ice and the skipper and his party had seen all in the wrecked boat get onto the ice with their luggage.

Then the fog had shut down again and Captain Karofsen had been unable to find the castaways. He had returned to Reykjavik and was now ready, if furnished with necessary funds, to get up a searching party and start after the lost men.

"It would be weeks before we could hear from such a searching party," groaned Mr. Swift. "What will you tell Mary and her mother, Tom?"

"Don't tell 'em anything," advised Ned. "Wait until we hear something for sure."

But this could not be. It was impossible to hide the facts from Mary Nestor. Before Tom had got out of bed, after spending most of the night at the telephone, Rad knocked on his door.

"Miss Mary come, Mars' Tom," said the old darkey through the keyhole. "She done got a letter from her father."

"Great Scott!" exclaimed Tom, getting out of bed in a hurry. "He can't have got off that iceberg and written her, all as quickly as this!"

He did not stop to dress, but put on his blanket robe and went downstairs. Mary was talk-

ing with Mr. Swift and had already got an ink-
ling of the trouble. She was very pale and her
eyes glistened with tears.

"Oh, Tom! what shall we do?" she cried, when
the young inventor appeared. "We never should
have let him go with Mr. Damon."

"Why not?" Tom demanded. "Isn't your
father better?"

"He says in this letter that he is. Much better. But that was written a month ago. It was
sent by the last mail steamer for the season.
Father and Mr. Damon should have taken that
steamer. But the legacy Mr. Damon went after
had not then been put into his hands. Think,
Tom! Thirty thousand dollars in Danish money
that his old friend, Aman Dele, left to him. The
priest had it hidden away in a vault under his little
stone church at Rosestone. Father tells us all
about it in this letter."

"Then they are only delayed up there in Iceland," began Tom rather faintly.

"Don't!" exclaimed Mary. "I know more than
that. Your father says they have been wrecked
at sea. I must know all, Tom," and Mary's eyes
filled with tears as she struggled courageously
for self-control.

"Oh, it may not be anywhere near as bad as
it seems," began Tom.

"But—but they *are* lost? Oh, Tom! What

shall we do? And what would I ever do without you, Tom? It startles me sometimes when I realize how much I depend on you."

"I'm glad you do, Mary."

"But what shall we do? It was so like Mr. Damon to try to reach Greenland in a small boat!"

"Not so small, I imagine. That *Kalrye* carried a crew of ten. A good-sized schooner. She probably ran into a ledge of ice just as the *Titanic* did, years ago. But the captain declares he saw his men and passengers safely on the iceberg."

"When was that?" Mary demanded, wiping her eyes and speaking more practically.

"About ten days ago. The captain had to work his way back to Reykjavik under sail in a whale boat."

"Could they live so long on an iceberg?"

"Why not if they had provisions? And the captain said the other boat carried both water and supplies."

"But they would have to remain on the ice until rescued!"

"Looks so," admitted Tom.

"If we started at once for Iceland it would be two months before we could get to Reykjavik, wouldn't it?" the girl asked.

Tom said nothing. His father exclaimed:

"My poor girl! Passenger service to the island is probably closed until spring."

"Then," said Mary Nestor firmly, "there is only one hope for father."

She looked straight at Tom, and he nodded slowly.

"Only one chance that I can see," he said.

It was the turn of Mr. Swift to be astonished.

"What do you two young people mean?" he asked.

Tom smiled slowly. "Mary gets the idea, dad," he said cheerfully. "I shall start for Iceland just as soon as possible. We will pick up Captain Karofsen, if he will go with us, to point out the iceberg where he left a part of his crew and the passengers marooned, and——"

"But how will you go? What route will you follow at this time of year?" Mr. Barton Swift demanded.

"We'll go on the wings of the wind," declared his son, laughing outright. "Of course, this eventuality is exactly what I must have built the *Winged Arrow* for. I will telephone the shops at once and tell Brannigan to get the crew together. I'll take Ned and Koku. If my new flying boat is any good at all, she ought to fly to Iceland in less than three days. As soon as she can be made ready, I will start, Mary."

"Oh, Tom! suppose you should be lost, too? Suppose you should be killed?"

"That can happen but once," declared Tom.

"Only once! But that's the horror of it! Oh, Tom!" and Mary gave a slight shudder.

"Let's not worry about that, Mary."

But both knew that Mary would carry a load of worry in her heart, and not entirely for her father.

CHAPTER XVI

THE TRANSATLANTIC VOYAGE

It was possible, of course, to cable funds to Captain Olaf Karofsen for the financing of a searching party to go in quest of those marooned on the giant iceberg. But Tom Swift knew that the result of such a search could not be known in the United States for weeks. He felt that he could not restrain his desire to take an active part in the search. Mary's father and Mr. Wakefield Damon must be found soon. And he believed the best way to do this was to go personally with the searching party.

Mr. Swift might have had some objections to his son's plan. He was getting old, and, although his health now was much improved, he worried whenever Tom left him for any extended trip.

In this case, however, he knew the young fellow felt strongly that his duty lay in the only chance of quickly assisting Mr. Nestor. The *Winged Arrow* had proved her speed, her seaworthiness, and her balance in the air. If she was good for anything at all, here was a set of circumstances seemingly made by Fate for the trying-out of the flying boat.

"Go if you must, my boy," said the old gentleman, with his hand on Tom's shoulder when he agreed to the arrangement. "But be very, very careful."

Although Tom was courageous, he was never reckless. He had accepted Mary's challenge on the instant. But it was not without thought.

"The moment I read that cablegram from Karofsen I saw what it meant," he told Ned. "The *Winged Arrow* can go where no vessel can sail. If she arrives at Reykjavik in good condition, she can sweep the whole of the Greenland Sea, back and forth, until the berg on which the men were cast away is found. If Karofsen is honest——"

"That is a chance, too," retorted Ned. "It looks fishy to me, Tom."

"What looks fishy?"

"His story. He knew all about that treasure of more than a hundred and twenty thousand Danish crowns. Humph! Suppose he and some of his crew got up a scheme to grab the gold and pitch those who were not in their confidence, as well as the passengers, overboard? Looks fishy."

"You sound mighty suspicious. And it might be so. Anyway, how are we going to prove even such an awful thing if we can't be on the ground——"

"Huh! On the ice would sound better," grumbled Ned.

"All right. Whichever way you wish to put it. Anyway, if we let the thing go on until next spring any crime of the character you suggest would be well covered up. I am going to get there as soon as the wings of the wind will take me."

His decision, which he communicated to Captain Olaf Karofsen by cable, must have amazed that individual immensely. Tom cabled two hundred dollars through a Danish-American bank for the captain's use until Tom himself arrived in Reykjavik.

"Expect me on Friday," was the concluding sentence of Tom's cablegram to the skipper of the wrecked *Kalrye*. That day was three days following the date of the cablegram. Later it was proved that the message shook society in the Icelandic port to its very foundations.

The fact that the new flying boat was about to start upon a flight into the Arctic could not be kept out of the newspapers, for the crew had to be told where they were going if they stuck to their jobs. And not one of the mechanicians refused to take part in the expedition.

Besides, Koku was to go. Rad Sampson

scoffed openly at this. He knew well enough that he could not go himself. He must stay and take care of Mr. Swift. But the old colored man refused to acknowledge that Koku could be of any possible use up near the Arctic Circle.

"Mus' be, Mars' Tom, you is wantin' to weight down dat flying boat so she can't eben rise out o' de sea. Dat big chunk of meat won't be no good to yo' lessen yo'-all uses him fo' an anchor."

"Whuf!" snorted Koku. "Koku great man. Koku fight!"

"See here, big boy," returned Rad, "yo'll have a hot time fightin' icebergs an' polar bears. Won't be much else fo' yo' to fight—no, sir."

However, the giant was proud indeed to be one of the party booked for a transatlantic passage heretofore never tried. The newspapers made much of it. In the sheets issued the day following the announcement of Tom's determination there were photographs of the crew of the *Winged Arrow,* and prominent in the group was Koku, dressed in the violently checked suit that had been given him by the president of the Hendrickton & Pas Alos Railroad.

Beside Koku, who could actually be called a member of the working crew of the *Winged Arrow,* Ned Newton had announced his intention of being of the party.

"If the inventor and head of the Swift Construction Company risks his life in such a venture, the treasurer of the concern might as well go along," Ned declared. "If you are lost, Tom Swift, there will be no company, so my job as treasurer won't be worth much. Count me in."

In like manner Kingston, the wireless operator, asked for a berth in the cabin of the seaplane. Tom really was touched by these expressions of loyalty and good will.

"Mary is crazy to go, as well!" he said, with a laugh. "But Mrs. Nestor vetoed the proposition and saved me from doing so. Mary has pluck enough to go."

Two hours before the time set for the flying boat's departure the inventor was astonished by still another application for passage on the *Winged Arrow*. It was a request signed by Rear Admiral Gilder, of the Naval Board, asking Tom Swift to allow a representative of that Board to accompany the party which the Admiral understood was about starting for Iceland. A representative, with full credentials from Washington, was on the way to Shopton.

"What do you suppose this means?" Tom demanded of Ned, who was his only confidant in this event. "I have had no correspondence with any Government official about the boat. I know Rear Admiral Gilder by name, but——"

"I bet you it is the French looking chap we marked down!" cried Ned eagerly.

"You think he represented the Naval Board and was spying about for them?" asked Tom, with much doubt.

"Who else could he be?"

"He could be almost anybody else," declared Tom, shaking his head. "He was too foreign looking to please me. And if he is the representative the Admiral sends I shall not let him aboard in any case."

"Maybe the Government will buy the plane at a big price," suggested Ned, with some eagerness.

"Nobody will get a chance to buy it—not yet," Tom rejoined firmly. "And there is something queer about this request, I tell you. It does not look right. There is no time now to find out about it. We shall be in the air, I hope, before this representative, whoever he is, arrives at Shopton. Not even the Naval Board can delay our departure in this instance. Every hour is precious."

Tom was not entirely correct in his expectation. While the last preparations were being made a powerful motor-car came into the open lot behind the shops from which point the flying boat was about to take its flight. The man who got briskly out of the enclosed tonneau of the car was exactly the individual both Tom and Ned had in mind—the dressy individual with the Charlie Chaplin mustache and diminutive goatee!

The man ran through the throng that had gathered to watch the jump-off. He bore several papers in his hands and he shouted to the boys whom he saw in the windows of the prow of the ship.

"Monsieur Swift! Monsieur Newton! Hi!"

"Hi yourself," growled Ned. "There's the fellow, Tom."

Tom gave the stranger a single glance and then spoke to Koku:

"Stand by the open door, Koku. Let nobody in over the gangplank but the crew. Understand?"

"Me understand, master," said the giant, and immediately stationed himself at the top of the narrow gangplank near the stern which was about to be drawn inboard.

When the stranger with the papers came to the plank the giant waved him commandingly away. The man started to argue. He might as well have argued with a stone post. Koku could not understand a word of English when he felt that way! Nor did any other language sound right, although the man tried French, German, and several other tongues. Koku was deaf.

When the supposed representative of the Naval

Board tried to advance up the plank, the giant stooped, raised both plank and man, and shook the latter off to the ground as though he had been a beetle.

Then the last of the crew came aboard and Koku drew in the plank and closed the door. Every other arrangement had been made. The propellers began to spin. The hawsers had been cast off. The great flying boat began bumping over the field.

They could not hear the foreign looking fellow's voice, but they saw that he ran after the flying boat, screaming, for several hundred yards. Then the *Winged Arrow* gathered speed enough for her jump-off, and she rose heavily, slanting upward at a good pitch, and wheeled away toward the sea.

"If that fellow does represent a Government Bureau, we'll hear about it when we get back," said Ned, somewhat worried.

"Don't bother your head about that," rejoined Tom. "There are more anxieties than that on my mind."

Tom had bidden good-bye to Mary Nestor and her mother early that morning.

"Bring him back to me, Tom," Mrs. Nestor had murmured, through her tears.

"I know you will do your best, Tom, dear," whispered Mary.

"I'll do my best for you, Mary," replied Tom softly. And he lingered a little over his good-bye to the girl, even though they both realized the need for haste.

Had the young inventor needed any inspiration for the journey, he would have gained it from the thought that these two helpless women were utterly dependent upon his good offices and that they believed he would be able to find and rescue the castaways on the giant iceberg.

The venture was one that was bound to bring to the surface of Tom Swift's character all his better and braver qualities. He did not take this trip in the big flying boat without fully understanding what he was likely to be up against before he returned home—if, indeed, he safely made the return!

Twenty-four hours before, he had made up his mind to take the journey. During that time he had put every agency at his disposal at work to the end that the party should be amply provisioned and well secured against accident of every kind.

Of course, fresh supplies of gasoline and oil could be obtained at Reykjavik. Food, as well, could be bought there. But the young inventor did not leave Shopton and home without seeing personally that every man with him was well clothed, that in the cabin there were all the simple medical remedies usually supplied to a sailing ship, and that there were arms and ammunition for every man.

Koku insisted on bringing his long spear and a great war club. Ned wanted to forbid this display of savage implements, but Tom allowed his servant to bring the weapons in the use of which he was versed.

"Those Icelanders will think we are American aborigines instead of civilized beings," grumbled Ned.

"I reckon the polar bears will not criticize Koku's selection of weapons," chuckled Tom. "I've seen Koku catch a charging jaguar on the point of that spear in mid-air and impale it as you would stick a beetle with a pin. And one crack with that war club would knock over a walrus, I believe. Let him alone, Ned."

"Humph!" said Ned. "You are quite sure, are you, that we shall search the Greenland Sea for Mr. Damon and Mr. Nestor? You thoroughly believe Skipper Karofsen's report?"

"Give him the benefit of the doubt," said Tom placidly. "You can scarcely judge a man's character by his cablegrams."

Discussion was mostly barred, however, when the *Winged Arrow* was well up and away from her base. They followed a slightly different course to the ocean line than they had on the trial

trip. On the chart table Tom Swift had thumb-
tacked a brand new map and had plotted out their
course from the vicinity of Shopton to the principal seaport of Iceland.

The direction was almost exactly north of east.
It would take the flying boat over the great fishing banks south of Newfoundland, across the
northern, or summer, route of the transatlantic
steamships, and over the lonely reaches of that
great northern ocean on which at this season of
the year drifted countless icebergs.

Ned studied the course as closely as Tom had
previously done. "If Mr. Damon and Mr. Nestor
started for Greenland to catch a steamer, how is
it Karofsen reports that they were wrecked in the
Greenland Sea?" he asked. "That is north of
Iceland. The most direct route to the Greenland
coast from Reykjavik is across Denmark Strait."

"I guess the only town from which fish is
shipped south is on what they call the Liverpool
Coast," his friend replied. "You will see that
that section of Greenland is across Greenland Sea.
If the current sets toward the south, however,"
Tom added, "this gigantic iceberg that Karofsen
tells about may be drifting into Denmark Strait.
That being the case, it may possibly narrow our
search."

Ned merely grunted in rejoinder. Even if they
reached Iceland safely in the flying boat, he had

grave doubts as to their ever finding a "chunk of ice," as he expressed it, floating around in the Arctic seas with seven men upon it and a treasure chest containing more than a hundred and twenty thousand Danish crowns!

When the flying boat crossed the line of the seacoast and flew out over the Atlantic it was plain that the sea had gone down. When they were well out from the shore the surface of the water seemed as smooth as a mill pond.

But, smooth or rough, Tom hoped that he would not be obliged to descend in the seaplane until the *Winged Arrow* arrived at her destination. He had taken every precaution, he believed, for the long and arduous flight. The speed at which they traveled encouraged him to believe that his hope would be realized.

As they went on, flying so high that shipping on the sea could only be distinguished through the glass, the atmosphere became very cold. They were getting farther away from the source of earth heat and the thermometer fastened outside one of the windows of the pilot room showed a rapid decline of the fluid.

Every man aboard the great flying boat had been dressed in warm clothing—the batten-lined leather suits of the ordinary flying men—when they left the ground. But Tom had furnished fur coats and hoods and gloves for them all.

Their boots were sheepskin lined. Water began to freeze inside the boat; but the crew kept warm.

Their breath began to congeal upon the inside of the windows and Ned spent most of his time cleaning the glass with alcohol. Kingston at first had sent news of the flight by wireless; but now the altitude and the temperature interfered with the working of the radio. Static made the sending and receiving of messages all but impossible.

The member of the crew who acted as cook brought coffee and sandwiches into the cabin and reported that the electric heaters did not work as well as previously and that it was difficult to boil water.

"We are up pretty high," Tom admitted; "but I believe if I scale her down much we shall be buffeted a good deal by head winds. We are making excellent time as she is. If we can stand the cold until nightfall——"

"Go ahead," replied Ned. "I might as well be a frozen turnip as the way I am," he grumbled. "Do you see Iceland yet?"

"I'll wake you up when I see Olaf Karofsen smoking his pipe on the dock at Reykjavik," scoffed Tom.

It was cold! And the idea of waiting until nightfall before dropping to a lower altitude was found not to be feasible. In the first place, they had flown into the region of long twilight. Darkness did not come until near midnight.

The *Winged Arrow* had by that time flown more than a thousand miles. Her inventor did not push her to her top-notch speed, but the time she made was perfectly satisfactory.

Crew and officers of the flying boat stood watch and watch, as on shipboard. Tom could not be at the controls all of the time, and he slept at least two full four-hour watches during the flight. But he was in charge when, late the following day, a hazy spot on the sea ahead announced the presence of land.

The perfectly adjusted instruments with which the pilot room in the prow of the flying boat was supplied had enabled them to keep on almost a direct course for Iceland. There could be no mistake in this. As she drew nearer and Tom pitched her nose on a downward slant, they saw the white horses of the surf breaking against the rockbound shore of the great island.

They spied a cluster of houses and several church spires on the southwestern coast, and steered for that point.

"Reykjavik," declared Tom Swift.

"I thought that must be on the north side of the island if that wrecked schooner started across Greenland Sea," remarked Ned.

"They passed along the western and northern

coast of the island before pushing out for Liverpool Coast," announced his friend. "At any rate, that schooner captain must be a pilot for these seas, and knows his business. The thing that troubles me is, will he go with us in the *Winged Arrow?* He may be afraid."

"We'll kidnap him, then, and make him go," declared Ned warmly. "We haven't come all this way to be balked like that, I should hope!"

CHAPTER XVII

"SOMETHING ROTTEN IN DENMARK"

THE *Winged Arrow* spiraled above the Icelandic port until she was so close to the ground that all landmarks could be easily distinguished. There were open fields behind the town, and Tom marked one of these cleared spaces for his landing.

They saw a good part of the inhabitants of Reykjavik trooping out of the town toward the place where it was evident the huge flying boat would make her landing. Tom and his crew were so much engaged in the work of bringing down the plane that at first the nature of the throng hurrying out from the town did not impress itself upon their attention.

The *Winged Arrow* swooped and rebounded from her wheels. The truck groaned and the tail of the boat began to drag. Her speed was soon brought down, she halted, Koku slid back the main door in the hull of the boat and was about to thrust out the narrow gangplank.

But Ned had spied something that the others

had not at first noted. Marching in the van of the crowd from town were about two dozen uniformed men bearing rifles on their shoulders.

"Seems to me," said Ned, pointing out this military party, "the Iceland militia may want to interfere with our landing, Tom. What say?"

"A warm reception, is it?" asked Kingston, sticking his head out of the radio coop.

"Hold on!" cried Tom, beckoning to Koku. "Don't let anybody get aboard yet, boy."

Koku dropped the end of the gangplank and in a couple of strides reached his long spear and war club. When he appeared at the open door again his appearance was, to say the least, rather warlike.

The military, or policemen, or whatever they were, warned the boys back, and most of the men and women remained at a safe distance from the flying boat. But one excited individual, who seemed to have some influence with the squad of soldiers, pushed up close to the seaplane and began to shout.

"If the only language they use here is the kind that old friend of Mr. Damon's tried to use in New York," said Ned, who had heard about Aman Dele's troubles, "we'll have a sweet time learning what they want or making them understand what we want."

"Of course many folks on the island understand

English," declared Tom, and went to the open door which Koku so savagely guarded.

"This is the flying boat from America—yes?" asked the excited man in broken English.

"Were you expecting two?" asked Tom, chuckling. "I guess this is she."

"I represent the Soviet Government," was the man's next astonishing declaration. "By cablegram I was told to expect this flying wonder. You and your crew, Captain, may land. I take charge of the flying boat from now on. It is arranged to send her on to Russia with our own men."

"To Russia?" gasped Tom Swift. "You represent the Bolshevist Government of Russia?"

"The Soviet Government—yes. The Governor of Reykjavik has agreed to allow the exchange to be made here——"

"Nonsense!" broke in the young inventor. "Either you are out of your mind, or somebody has been fooling you. I built this flying boat myself and I have no intention of selling it to Russia or any other country."

"What is that? You deny that our representative, Monsieur Polansky, bought this flying boat and cabled me to take it over when it landed here?"

"You are crazy!" exclaimed Tom Swift, in disgust. He beckoned to the uniformed officer in command of the military force. "Do you speak English?" he cried.

"But yes, Monsieur. Speak slowly. I can understand you," said the officer.

"Then understand me right now," Tom said, with emphasis. "This fellow who says he represents Russia, has absolutely nothing to do with this flying boat."

"No? But he has writings from the Governor——"

"I am here," interrupted Tom, in firm tones, "to search for two friends—Mr. Damon and Mr. Nestor—who were lost from the wreck of the motor schooner *Kalrye*. Do you understand me? Where is Captain Olaf Karofsen?"

"I do not understand!" cried the officer anxiously. "I am instructed to take charge of this machine until the Russian official brings his crew to sail her away."

"You will not take charge of my flying boat, and no bunch of Russian Reds will ever get hold of it!" declared Tom warmly. "I begin to smell the rat in this meal bin," he added over his shoulder to Ned.

"What is it? Oh! That Frenchy who was so anxious to come with us?"

"Bet you a copper cent!" ejaculated Tom. "But he was no Frenchman. A Russian!" Then to the disturbed officer of the Danish squad he said: "Better send this Soviet Consul, or whatever he is, home with a flea in his ear. We are on an important mission, and if we are interfered with I will send for Mr. Shantuck, the representative of the United States. You know him?"

"Quite so, Monsieur," said the officer, who evidently understood French better than he did English, and of which language Tom Swift could speak a few words. "But this gentleman——"

"He has absolutely nothing to do with my flying boat," declared the young inventor. "See! Who is that coming?"

He had caught sight of a figure almost as tall as Koku's pushing its way through the crowd of interested spectators. Tom had noticed that there were many tall men in the throng, but this person was head and shoulders above most of them. He was heavily bearded and wore a knitted jersey and cap, as some foreign sailors do.

"This may be your Captain Karofsen," said the military officer.

The burly giant who approached swiftly impressed Tom on nearer view most favorably. While the self-styled representative of the Soviet Government sputtered to the military officer, the big sailor came close to the side of the seaplane.

"Misder Swift—yes?" he said in a deep voice. "When I got telegram you come in t'ree days I say: 'Das American come t'roo de air—yes?'

Undt, py jolly! so he came—yes. I sail to America once, twice. So I spe'k de English goot."

"You surely do, Captain," declared Tom delightedly, realizing that this man was too simple a soul to have entered into any plot against Mr. Damon and Mr. Nestor. "But it looks as if we might have trouble if we stop here for long."

"Vot trouble iss dot?" demanded Captain Karofsen.

Tom explained briefly about the claim made by the Red who still gabbled angrily to the military officer. He was threatening to call upon the Governor of Reykjavik to reiterate an order to seize the seaplane.

"And we must get some more gasoline before we try to find that iceberg," concluded Tom.

"Yes—I see," agreed Captain Karofsen. "You go find Misder Damon undt the sick man with this flying boat? I been trying to charter one sailing boat—yes."

"What do you think? You'll go with us, won't you?"

"Jes. She peat all de sailing poats in de vorl'," cried the captain emphatically. "I see her sail down out of the skies, so like von bird. Wonderful!"

"But the gasoline?"

"Gasoline we shall buy at a station on the north coast of Iceland. A Standard Oil tanker bane stop dere twice in de year now—yes. You pay me for my time, Misder Swift?"

"I surely will. You will lose nothing by going to help us," cried Tom.

"I go. I gif you back de eight hunder' gold crowns you send me undt you pay me my captain's wages like I have before de *Kalrye* she was sink. Eh?"

"A bargain!" declared Tom. "When do we go?"

"Let dat big man give me de hand up, and we start now," answered Skipper Karcfsen placidly. "When dat man down dere want to make trouble we will not be here. Ja—yes?"

The coolness of this proposition delighted Ned immensely; and Tom was satisfied that it would be the best and wisest way out of the difficulty. He did not intend to be delayed here if he could help it.

"Guess we'd better take his tip and go," Tom remarked with a questioning look at Ned.

"As Shakespeare once wrote, 'there is something rotten in Denmark,'" rejoined Ned, in a low voice, peering out at the excited Bolshevist. "If the Island authorities wish to call us to account for what we do, we'd better hunt for the castaways first. Come aboard, Captain Karofsen."

Tom motioned to Koku, who dropped his spear

and club and stooped to seize the other giant's wrist. Koku lifted and Captain Karofsen heaved himself up with surprising agility. Without using the gangplank he reached the sill.

"Mark the place we shall stop for gasoline on that chart, Captain," said Tom, pointing to the chart table.

The next moment he signaled Brannigan to start the motors. The flying boat began to quiver throughout her length. They were about to make the jump-off.

CHAPTER XVIII

THE GIANT BERG

THE first movement of the big flying boat attracted the attention of the crowd of onlookers as well as the soldiery and the excited civilian that had put in such a ridiculous claim for possession of Tom Swift's newest invention. Those gathered in the pilot room of the seaplane could see everyone hurrying to get out of the expected course of the *Winged Arrow*.

"We'll settle that fellow's hash when we come back," declared Tom, shaking his head, as he glanced out at the stranger.

"*If* we come back, you mean," replied Ned. "And take it from me, Tom, that chap is linked up with the French fellow that bothered us before we left Shopton."

"Looks so. But that Polansky, as this chap called him, was no Frenchman, I tell you."

"Doesn't matter. He had an awful amount of nerve," said Ned. "Now we're rising!"

The seaplane took the air as nicely as she had

before. Captain Olaf Karofsen was tracing the course they should follow across Iceland. The place to which he directed Tom for gasoline was a small whaling port facing the stretch of Arctic Ocean called the Greenland Sea.

The long twilight of this northern clime made the journey really a pleasant one. Tom, to avoid air currents caused by the mountains, veered a little and skirted a shoulder of Mount Hekla, from the crater of which a thin column of smoke was rising. The captain told them there had been no eruption of the ancient volcano since he was a child, but it was not entirely cold.

Captain Karofsen was much more interested in the management of the seaplane, however, than he was in the physical wonders of Iceland. The boys were eager to know the particulars of the wreck of the *Kalrye* and how Mr. Damon and Mr. Nestor had been thrown upon the iceberg.

"I lost das schooner—yes," said the captain, shaking his head. "Das insurance don't pay me for all. And if them gentlemen are lost for good, I never get over it."

It seemed that in the night and fog two monstrous peaks of ice loomed up ahead of the *Kalrye,* but so many miles away that the captain and crew of the schooner had no idea their boat would collide with the berg.

She had run bow on to a ledge, and with a

heavy sea following her, the stiff hull of the
schooner was battered into wreckage in a very
few minutes. The two boats were got safely out
and the crew divided. Both boats were well provisioned. The one in which the two passengers
sailed with their treasure and baggage was badly
managed. A billow caught up the craft and threw
her broadside upon the ice.

"She vas smashed like you step on von cock-
roach," groaned Karofsen. "But dark as it vos,
I see all the party high and dry. They signal us
with flashlight. We tell them we go for help—
yes. It was the best we could do."

"I believe you," agreed Tom. "And if you are
sure you can pick out the same berg——"

"Jes! It vos so pig a perg—yes. I could not
be mistaken. And those great spires of ice, side
by side! Fear not, Misder Swift, I bane sure
of it."

"Do you feel quite sure that they are still
alive, Captain?" Tom asked.

"They haf food—yes. They may freeze, but
they do not starve. And if they haf sense they
save wreckage from the boat to make fire. Ja!"

"At any rate," Tom said more cheerfully to his
chum, "it's a chance."

"Well, I suppose so. But you yourself look
out how you go sailing around over these icebergs.
If you break a wing or a propeller or anything,

and we drop on to a field of ice ourselves, we'll be as bad off as Mr. Damon and Mr. Nestor."

From the height at which the seaplane sailed across the island, heading north now, the travelers could see a vast expanse of the Arctic sea. The sun was so low on the horizon that its beams gave little light. But the sky seemed overcast with a luminous haze and under that the sea, and what floated upon it, was clearly visible.

Countless little crackling points of dull fire revealed the presence of broken ice. Here and there a spire, or hummock, rose to a considerable height from the surface. Tom Swift and his friends began to realize for the first time just what a search for a particular iceberg in these cold regions might mean.

They were utterly dependent on Captain Olaf Karofsen, it seemed. If he failed to remember how the berg looked on which he had last seen the marooned party of sailors and passengers, it would be very difficult for the searchers to find them.

"Looking for a needle in a haystack wouldn't be in it!" exclaimed Ned.

Captain Karofsen took Tom's glasses and peered steadily at the shore line ahead. He spied out at last the little collection of houses he had in mind, and Tom slightly changed the course of the seaplane to more nearly hit the port.

There was a breakwater and fishing boats; and at one point a tall staff which they soon made out to be rigged with wireless antennæ. Late as it was in the evening (nearly midnight now) they saw the inhabitants of the fishing port moving about. As the flying boat dropped lower, it was plain that there was some excitement below.

The great gasoline tanks were built on an iron bridge over the water and inside the breakwater. Captain Karofsen said there was plenty of hose with which the tank of the seaplane could be connected with the supply tank. There was an open field on the edge of the water where the flying boat might be brought down in safety.

But the sight of that wireless outfit had made Tom a little suspicious. Instead of sweeping down at once to the land, he shot the great boat out to sea, and then headed back again, facing the gas tanks. The pool of water inside the breakwater was fairly smooth.

"I see some more of those armed and uniformed men there," he said to Captain Karofsen. "We left Reykjavik without permission of the authorities. If your governor is one of those pompous fellows, he like enough has wirelessed an order over here to arrest us if we come down for gasoline."

"He could do dot," agreed the schooner captain, wagging his shaggy head like a nodding mandarin.

"I am going to drop inside the breakwater," Tom said quickly. "I can see there is room there. And we can make our jump-off all right after filling the tank. Ned, pass the guns to the crew; but no ammunition. We may have to make a show of force, but of course there must be no shooting."

"Master, let Koku go ashore," cried the giant. "Him dribe um off with his spear."

Captain Karofsen seemed much impressed by the savageness of Koku.

"I pet you him undt me could clean oudt the whole town. But Misder Swift, you no be troubled. Them polize don't fight yet unless the governor make 'em. They for what you call show—yes?"

"That is all right," laughed Tom. "But I, for one, have a hearty respect for the police of any country. Let's get this gasoline without any fight, if we can."

With the drumming of the motors stopped, the flying boat sank to the surface of the water almost in silence. By a patent arrangement, almost as soon as the plane was on even keel one of the airtight pontoons which were affixed to either end of the wings was detached and drawn in to an open door in the hull of the great craft.

This small boat was driven by a detachable motor. There was room in the cockpit for Tom and Koku and Captain Karofsen, but it was a tight fit! They pushed off immediately for the beach under the gasoline tanks.

The inhabitants of the port were gathered in a wondering group just above high water mark. They were mostly fishermen and their wives and children. There were six of the uniformed police, and their spokesman immediately advanced with a blue paper in his hand.

He spoke in a language which Tom did not understand, but which Captain Karofsen was familiar with. The schooner captain answered angrily. Then he said to Tom:

"This big walrus make de same demandt—yes. They are all crazy yet. I bane have a goot mind to slap him. He says we steal the seaplane."

"What does he want to have us do with it?" asked the inventor.

"Pring it ashore," and Karofsen laughed.

"Tell him we have to have gasoline before we can move it at all. Get the gasoline. That is the first thing to do."

Captain Karofsen, much amused, proceeded to convince the people ashore that the seaplane was immovable without a supply of gasoline. Tom had money with which to pay for what he needed, and after about half an hour's wrangling the hose was connected to the *Winged Arrow's* tank and a good supply of gasoline pumped aboard.

The small boat was then withdrawn from the beach and Tom and the two giants got into the hull of the plane. The airtight boat was coupled to the end of the wing again and they prepared for flight.

If the police of the fishing port expected to see the huge machine jump over the oil tanks and land on the beach, they were mistaken. When she took to the air, Tom swerved her in a half circle and she shot out over the sea again and soared into the darkening sky at railroad speed!

A sprinkle of brilliant stars had now appeared. The dome of the sky was like a deep blue velvet robe, all trimmed with sparkling sequins. On the horizon flashes of purple, scarlet, and green denoted the distant Aurora Borealis. It was a perfect Arctic night.

Tom sailed his flying boat not far above the water and ice. Vast sheets of the latter gleamed below the flying boat and they could trace long canals between the fields. Here and there rose the peak of a great berg.

"When you consider that only about one-seventh of the bulk of a berg is above the surface of the water, some of those fellows must be extraordinary in size," Tom said to Ned and Kingston.

"Some icebergs, I'll say!" murmured the wire-less operator. "And there are thousands of them. How are you ever going to pick up the one those folks were wrecked on?"

But Tom had already thought seriously of that point. The chart and Captain Karofsen agreed that the set of the current was southward between Greenland and Iceland, through the wide Denmark Strait.

"In all probability that berg our friends are on has been carried into the strait by this time," Tom declared.

"You seem dreadfully certain that the poor chaps are still alive," Ned said.

"Captain Karofsen has hope of that, so why not?" rejoined Tom. "We have not come away over here to find Mr. Damon and Mary's father starved or frozen, I hope."

But Tom was anxious. He would not leave his post in the pilot room that night. As the darkness increased the two great searchlights of the seaplane flashed their beams over the ice-fields, and it did seem as though, if there were any castaways there, these signals would be an-swered. The castaways from the *Kalrye* were known to have electric torches.

Until the thin edge of the sun appeared above the horizon again the *Winged Arrow* soared over the sea. Captain Karofsen pointed out the coast of Greenland, which the boys at first had thought was a row of icebergs in the distance.

"My *Kalrye,* she vos sailing by there when she vos wrecked," said the schooner captain. "We make it in about two days more. Undt she iss lost!"

The plane swept around and drifted back toward Iceland on the other tack. Beneath, the points of broken ice began to sparkle, tipped by the brief rays of the sun. The sheets of unbroken ice were as blue as the sea itself. As the plane moved southward there were fewer open channels and pools. It seemed, before noon, as though able men cast away in this ice might make their way to one shore or the other.

Yet, if they did, neither the Greenland nor Iceland coasts afforded much hope of succor. The first named was utterly barren for hundreds of miles, while the fishing settlements on Iceland were far apart on this northwestern coast.

Now and again somebody spied something moving on the ice, and down the flying boat would swoop that the object might be the better examined. In each case the searchers were disappointed. Several times small herds of seals were made out, or a pair of walruses. Once a huge polar bear was seen drifting down a channel, enthroned on a lump of ice. It had evidently been fishing at the edge of the open water and the chunk of ice had broken away from the parent field.

A school of round-backed whales, some ten of them, were observed swimming down a channel, evidently making for the warmer seas.

"Let Mr. Damon and his party catch one of those whales or a bear, and they'll be fixed all right for food," said Ned, chuckling. "Wouldn't Mr. Damon be blessing everything in nature if he came to eating blubber?"

Tom drove his flying boat first to the east until they could see the coast of the big island they had left the night before, and then turned her about and drove west until Greenland was in sight. At each lap he brought their course many miles southward. Little floating on the surface of the sea escaped their keen gaze.

It was mid-afternoon when Captain Olaf Karofsen, looking through Tom's powerful glasses, began to show more excitement. Even with only the naked eye there could be seen ahead two tall pinnacles like cathedral towers. There was a narrow space between them, and miles upon miles of hummock ice and low bluffs lay about the two spires.

"Dot iss she!" exclaimed Captain Karofsen. "I vould not fool you, Misder Swift. Dot is de perg I see Mr. Damon and the sick man undt my five sailors from the *Kalrye* climb upon when their boat was smashed. I could not mistake those two points like chimneys."

"Is there anything moving on that great field of ice?" demanded Tom anxiously.

His companions used their eyes, and the binoculars, as well, to the best advantage. Tom drove the flying boat nearer and nearer to the pinnacles of ice. Not a moving object was descried beneath them. The great iceberg seemed to be as abandoned as any of the other fields they had flown over during their marvelous journey through the air.

CHAPTER XIX

THE DESERT OF ICE

THE portion of the great iceberg that was visible consisted of a good many square miles of hills and valleys of ice, with the two more important eminences standing close together near the middle of the vast field.

It was so huge that its movement (and bergs are always in motion) could not be observed at all. It seemed as immovable as the island of Iceland itself, yet Captain Olaf Karofsen was positive that it had drifted a good many miles southward during the two weeks since his schooner had been wrecked on one of the outer reefs of the berg.

As the *Winged Arrow* swooped lower, and Tom Swift drove it around the entire outer edge of the iceberg, the schooner captain tried to mark the spot where the *Kalrye* had struck and sunk and the spot where the lifeboat had been smashed.

There was not a scrap of either wreck to be seen. The changing surface of the ice offered no certain mark of any party of castaways having been upon it. The seaplane circumnavigated the huge berg twice with the same result. The hearts of Tom and Ned failed them. They feared that the disaster had been wholly tragic, after all.

But Captain Karofsen would not give up hope. He pointed out that his five sailors were all seasoned men, used to the Arctic, and of wide experience. First of all, he said, they would have saved the boat, cut it up with the boat axes, and transported it and the provisions to some sheltered place on the berg.

"There be hunderts of caves—yes? Many, many places for to hide and keep varm. Iceland men don't gif up so easy, Misder Swift."

It was plain to be seen that there were many valleys and sheltered dens in the middle of the berg into which the crew of the seaplane could not see. The flying boat might pass back and forth over the iceberg a hundred times and not be spied by the castaways if they were thus holed up.

"But we do not even see any smoke," said Ned. "If they had a fire——"

"They would be careful with their fuel," interrupted Tom. "We might hang around up here for a couple of days and miss seeing anything of them if they are there——"

"A wise 'if,'" interrupted Ned.

"Unless they come out to hunt food——"

"Hoh!" cried Ned again. "Dig potatoes, I suppose?"

"Don't be foolish!" commanded Tom. "There are seals and bears, and Captain Karofsen says that both Mr. Damon and Mr. Nestor had rifles."

"That's right," agreed Ned. "I did not think of that."

"So," concluded Tom firmly, "I am going to descend into that middle valley——"

"Not between those two peaks, Tom?" cried his friend. "That is a bad hole to get out of."

"I mean the valley just beyond. See! Look close."

He managed the controls so that the great flying boat headed in between the tall pinnacles of ice. As they rushed into the narrow valley between the greenish-white walls of ice, they found the cleft much deeper than they had at first supposed. There was an unexpected draught through the passage, too.

The *Winged Arrow* swerved unexpectedly to one side, and her right wing scraped along the ice cliff. The plane was jarred from stem to stern and several cables snapped.

The collision dislodged a huge mass of the ice that came tumbling down, barely missing the tail of the boat and falling with a thunderous crash into the bottom of the gorge.

"You'd better get out of this, Tom!" yelled Ned. "Shoot her up!"

The passage between the ice cliffs was too narrow and crooked, however, for Tom to risk any abrupt ascent. Still rocking from the force of that slam against the ice, the seaplane staggered on, but at reduced speed. The valley was several miles long.

Again and yet again the end of one wing or the other touched the ice. These slight collisions did no particular harm, but they emphasized the fact that Tom could not govern the mechanism as perfectly as he had before.

The balance of the plane was overset. She was likewise sinking. When Tom signaled for a "lift," Brannigan could not work his levers properly. Like a huge wounded air fowl, the *Winged Arrow* fluttered lower and lower.

"My goodness, Tom! are we done for?" gasped his chum.

Tom's face was pale, but he did not lose his self-control. He dared not raise the nose of the flying boat sharply, for if he did and she then took a tail spin she would land upon her propeller and put that out of commission.

The craft continued to descend. Tom waved a disengaged hand toward the right hand window. Ned and the others saw what he wished to call their attention to.

The airtight pontoon at that end of the great wing had been smashed in the collision with the wall of ice and now hung partly disengaged from its proper fastenings. This had so disarranged the balance of the boat that her management was most difficult, especially in this narrow chasm.

Another sharp turn in the valley of ice loomed before them. Below, Tom saw that the bottom of the gorge was comparatively smooth for some distance. If they could make a fair landing, they might be able to repair the pontoon and then rise on even keel again.

He quickly signaled Brannigan, who shut down the motors. The roar of them ceased almost at once. The great flying boat sank to rest in the heart of the giant iceberg.

CHAPTER XX

IMPRISONED IN THE ICE

WHEN the throbbing of the motors ceased and the flying boat had stopped rebounding on its wheels and tail, the party in the pilot room stared at each other in a silence that was pregnant with anxiety. Even Koku, who stood on guard, felt that the situation of the *Winged Arrow* was serious; yet Koku believed that the "magic" of his Master Tom was equal to almost any emergency.

Tom as a usual thing had plenty of confidence in himself, and especially in his ability to get out of scrapes. But this was one event over which he seemed to have little control.

"What shall we do?" asked Ned.

"Got to find that out, I guess," admitted the young inventor. "First of all the boys will have to fix that pontoon. It's a mess. And without it in position the flying boat will be lopsided when I try to raise her."

"Great!" groaned Ned. "So we are marooned down here at the bottom of this hole in the ice?"

Tom went aft to confer with his mechanicians. Ned and Kingston got into their outer furs, lent an extra coat to Captain Karofsen, and the trio opened the door and by the aid of a light steel ladder got down upon the ice.

The gorge was not more than four hundred feet wide at this point, and the walls of ice towered above their heads at least a thousand feet. If they found it necessary to scale those heights afoot, it would be a difficult and perilous venture.

Tom and the mechanicians came piling out after a bit, and a close inspection was made of the airtight boat pendant from the right wing. It could be repaired, of course; but it necessarily would take considerable time.

"Go ahead," said Tom. "We have food and heat in plenty. Do your best, Brannigan. Meanwhile the rest of us will take a look through this cañon. I wonder if firing our rifles would attract the attention of Mr. Nestor and the others if they are near here."

"I tell you what it might do," said the wireless operator, Kingston.

"What's that?"

"It might bring down an avalanche of ice on our heads. You know a cracking stick has been known to start an avalanche."

"Gee!" exclaimed Ned. "I wish you didn't know so much. Why tell us that? I'll get a crick in my neck now, I know, watching out for the ice to fall."

But it was no joking matter. Kingston was right, as Tom well knew. Yet the young inventor felt that they should try as quickly as possible to find Mr. Damon and Mary's father. If the two were still on the giant iceberg it would be well if they were discovered soon. Tom had no desire to remain marooned at the bottom of this gorge for long.

Captain Karofsen was still cheerfully optimistic about finding his seamen and passengers from the wrecked *Kalrye*. There were thousands of places in the iceberg where they might conceal themselves. And unless by chance they had seen the seaplane flying over the berg, the castaways would never know that a searching party had come to look for them.

The schooner captain, however, agreed that it would be unsafe to fire the guns. At least, it must not be done down here in the maw of the iceberg.

"We bane look for them—yes? If they haf been here they must leave somet'ing behind. We see where they camp—yes?"

"Come on!" Tom sang out. "We would better keep together. No knowing what there may be on this berg besides castaways."

"Bears, for instance!" rejoined Ned Newton.

"Come on, Koku. Maybe that big spear of yours may be of some use yet."

The giant grinned and marched ahead with the spear poised for quick use. The party took up their march along the bottom of the gorge, leaving Brannigan and his helpers to repair the flying boat.

From above, as the flying boat had hovered over the ice peaks, the party had gained rather an unsatisfactory idea of what the gorge was like. But, of course, had it not been for the accident to the pontoon Tom would never have descended into the cañon between these towering, icy walls with his invention.

Beyond the place where the *Winged Arrow* had been forced to land there seemed to be several miles of the gorge, and it was by no means a straightaway cleft in the ice. It twisted and turned like the path of a tortured snake.

"We'd have a fat chance following this cañon in that flying boat," remarked Ned. "Quick as they got one thing repaired, we'd crash into a spur of this ice and crack something else. I tell you, Tom, just as soon as we can, we want to get up out of this hole."

"Reckon you are right," agreed his chum. "Hi! See there! What is it that Koku has found?"

The giant had suddenly increased his stride,

thrusting his spear forward and showing every evidence of excitement. He was several rods in advance of the remainder of the party. Tom and the others half expected to see somebody rise up to face the giant, but as they rounded a spur of ice and joined Koku there seemed to be nobody else in sight.

"What is it?" demanded Tom.

"Master see?" exclaimed the giant, and showed them what he had speared.

"Great Scott! A bean can!" cried Tom.

Ned burst into laughter. "Civilization—a sure mark!" he chortled. "Yankees have been here, you may be sure."

Tom turned to Captain Karofsen.

"How about it, Captain? There is the label still sticking to it. Was that a brand of beans included in the stores of the *Kalrye?*"

"That iss idt," rejoined the schooner captain. "They been here—yes. See that cave yonder, Misder Swift? Perhaps they have been there in that cavern."

Koku had already seen the opening of a considerable cavity in one wall of the gorge. He advanced cautiously. The cavern appeared to be very deep. It was dark beyond the entrance. As the party hesitated before the opening they could distinctly feel a draught of air blowing from the hole.

"It's a tunnel, I bet," said Ned. "What say? Think it goes clear through this ice mountain to the plain beyond?"

"Why not?" demanded Tom. "These ice cliffs seem honeycombed with such caves."

Koku suddenly shouted and darted forward into the mouth of the cave. There was a savage roar in reply—but it was no human voice that answered the giant's challenge.

"A bear!" exclaimed Tom, and he was first to follow the excited Koku into the half darkened cavity.

Ned was close on the young inventor's heels.

"Tom, do have a care!" he shouted.

"No time for care!" panted Tom. "Koku's fearless! No telling what he'll do!"

The giant thrust mightily with his spear and the challenging roar of the bear changed instantly to a scream of pain. With a crash of ice and breaking spear-handle, the huge beast appeared in the entrance to the cave.

Koku was overturned. He fell sprawling, with the broken handle still clutched in his mighty grip. The bear reared, plucking at the staff that impaled it. It stood taller than Captain Karofsen, or even Koku. It was a drab-white polar bear of fierce aspect, and its rumbling growls reverberated from the walls of ice, making a deafening clamor.

The schooner captain started forward, rifle raised, and in a moment flame darted from the muzzle of his weapon. The bear was hit—indeed, the captain could not have missed it—but it was not yet dead and fell back into the darkness of the cave.

They all advanced, holding their guns ready for another attack. Even Koku scrambled up and came on, brandishing his broken staff. It was fortunate indeed that the three young fellows and their two gigantic companions followed the wounded bear so closely.

Scarcely had the echoing explosion of Captain Karofsen's rifle died away when a mightier report sounded over their heads. Everybody halted, appalled. The peril of the wounded bear was forgotten. White-faced and motionless, they stared at one another. They all knew that something of vastly greater menace had occurred.

The explosion above was the breaking away of some overhanging shelf of ice. It came sliding and bursting down the face of the cliff and in half a minute was dumped with a terrific shock directly in the mouth of this cave which they had entered.

Powdered ice almost smothered the party for a few moments. Such light as there had been outside the cave in the cañon was snuffed out.

The avalanche crowded the cave's entrance and made the five explorers prisoners with a suddenness that stunned them all.

While from ahead, in the pitch darkness, came again the challenge of the wounded bear. It was by no means *hors-de-combat*. The wounded brute was full of fight. And to fire again in hope of killing the bear might bring the very roof of the ice cave down upon their heads!

CHAPTER XXI

A SILVER LINING

THE intense darkness inside the cave made the event a serious one. The wounded polar bear might charge among them at any moment, and as they were all dressed in furs it would be difficult to distinguish each other from the bear.

The bear uttered another terrific roar and charged from the back of the cave. Koku's war cry was almost as savage, and, knocking the others right and left, he sprang between his beloved master and the wild beast.

Tom, however, did not lose his self-possession. He was a little slow in getting it out, but he produced in time a flashlight, and the ray of it revealed the glaring eyes, the open, dripping jaws, and the blood-bedabbled breast of the big polar bear.

The blinding ray of electric light confused the animal and Koku reached him with several terrific whacks with the staff of his spear.

With one side swipe of its right paw the growl-

ing beast tossed the weapon away and drove
Koku to his knees. It reached with its left paw
to seize the giant, and the curved claws all but
caught him.

"Look out!" shrieked Ned. "He'll have you,
sure!"

Koku leaped up, but scarcely escaped the return swing of the bear's paw. Even the wind
of it was enough to send the man to the ice again.
With a blood-curdling roar the polar bear flung
himself forward on all four paws, and his shaggy
breast covered Koku.

It looked as though the faithful servant was
done for! His spear stuck a hand's breadth out
of the bear behind its shoulder. The blood
poured from that and from the gunshot wound
like muddy red bilge being pumped from a ship's
hold.

At this dreadful instant Olaf Karofsen flung
away his rifle, drew a great knife from his belt,
and leaped for the savagely wagging head of the
bear. It seemed as though he gave himself over
utterly to the jaws of the beast. The creature's
teeth snapped with a clash of ivory that sounded
well nigh as loud as had the rifle shot.

But the gigantic Icelander escaped the jaws.
He made a mighty downward thrust with the
skinning knife.

The point of it entered the bear's spine right

behind the skull and must have severed the first vertebra. The beast groaned with pain, weaving to and fro on its feet. For the moment all the fight was taken out of the animal. It shuddered and began to sink to the ice.

Uttering a great shout, Tom darted forward and seized Koku's shoulders. With Captain Karofsen's help he dragged Koku from under the dying bear. The huge body of the brute sunk slowly upon the very spot where Koku had lain. The giant could not have lived under the dead weight of the mountain of flesh.

Ned had picked up Tom's torch and now illumined the scene. The two giants were grinning at each other broadly. Tom spoke rather brokenly.

"I declare, boys, that was some fight! I'm proud of you, Koku. And how can I ever thank you, Captain Karofsen?"

The schooner captain was all seriousness again in a moment. He said to Tom:

"We nefer mind dot. The bear, he iss dead. But das snow and ice block us in here. We nefer dig out. We haf no tools."

Ned had turned the ray of the light upon the mass of broken ice that completely filled the mouth of the cavity into which they had ventured. From the sound of the avalanche when it fell, there could be little doubt but that the mass was rods thick. And the distance and force with which it had fallen had packed the shattered ice so tightly that there could be no hope of finding a passage through it.

"But, say!" exclaimed Kingston, when this fact had been discussed, "don't you fellows remember that there was a current of air blowing out of this cave when we stood before it? You mentioned that fact, Newton."

"I noticed it myself," Tom agreed quickly.

"So did I," added Ned.

"We haf no feel of de wind now," observed Captain Karofsen.

"Me look," cried Koku, who understood fully the situation and its attendant dangers. "If there be hole, I come back and tell Master."

"Hold on, Koku!" exclaimed Tom Swift. "I know you can pretty well see like a cat in the dark. But I think we had better stick together. We will all go with you on this search for another opening to the cave."

"Undt leaf das bear? Not even skin him? It is meat. We may need it," said the schooner captain, in some doubt.

"We have provisions for a week aboard the *Winged Arrow*," Tom said lightly.

"And one sure thing," supplemented Ned. "Nobody will get this bear if we leave it where it lies."

"But if we do not skin him while das body he iss warm, we haf a pad time doing so," declared the Icelander.

"I do not think we should bother with the bear," Tom said slowly. "I am worried about getting back to the seaplane. We may get through this cave and find outselves far up in these mountains of ice. We will have difficulty in lowering ourselves down into that gorge where the plane is. Don't bother with this bear. Let us go on."

"By jinks!" exclaimed Ned. "They say every cloud has a silver lining. It is so blamed dark right now that I cannot see any silver behind this cloud."

"Cheer up!" cried Tom, his own voice changing with an effort. "Lead ahead, Koku. Give me that torch, Ned. Look out where you step. There may be fissures here, or sink-holes, to fall into. Have a care, Koku."

"Me have much care, Master," said the faithful giant. "I feel wind again." He held up a finger he had wetted. "Yes. Wind come through big ice cave. We find um place to go out. Wait and see."

"I hope so," muttered Ned, as he came along in the rear of the small procession.

Farther back in the chamber in the ice was the entrance to a tunnel more than man-high. It was of considerable width, too, and when the party had entered it, almost at once the explorers found that the pitch of the floor was sharply upwards.

The tunnel was by no means straight, twisting around and around, and in places it proved to be open to the sky. There were deep clefts in the ice mountain that exposed the passage to the light of day.

Some of these cuts were deep with snow, for there had already been snow flurries in the Arctic Ocean from which this giant iceberg had drifted.

The explorers became quite hopeful as they pressed on, for it seemed as though finally there must be an exit to the tunnel. They spoke cheerfully together, but were somewhat worried over the fact that Brannigan and his mates would be disturbed by their delayed return.

"They won't know what to make of the delay," said Ned.

"But if they heard the avalanche—and of course they did—they may suspect what has happened to us," Tom remarked. "Hullo! What is it, Koku?"

The giant had halted and put out a restraining hand to stop those behind him. Tom shot the bright ray of the lamp ahead. He saw nothing, for there was a sharp turn in the passage there. They stood silent, waiting. The giant crept forward.

When the man-mountain reached the turn in the wall of ice, he stretched his neck around it. He stood so for so long that Tom went forward, too, making no noise. Almost at once, when he reached Koku's station, Tom heard a slight noise farther along the tunnel.

"Listen!" he whispered, and held up his hand for silence.

Was it an animal? Perhaps another bear? The young fellow unslung his rifle, for dangerous as it was to fire a weapon amid the towering ice, such another savage beast as that which had previously attacked them could only be met with powder and ball.

Koku flashed his master a quick glance. His wide mouth split his face in a grin. Something amused Koku immensely, but what it was Tom did not at first understand.

The others ventured forward until all stood in a group at the turn of the tunnel. Tom was listening again. The noise was repeated. Suddenly he swung about and slapped his chum on the shoulder.

"Ned," he whispered hoarsely, "you were saying there was no silver lining to this cloud of trouble! Don't you believe it! This is its silver lining. Listen!"

As he ceased speaking a hollow voice echoed along the passage:

"Bless the icicles on my mustache, this is the coldest house I ever lived in! The landlord should be prosecuted," and then the deep, bass laugh of Wakefield Damon reverberated in the ice-cleft.

"What do you know about this!"

"Here in the ice cave!"

"Come on and surprise them!"

At these words all rushed forward.

CHAPTER XXII

BACK TO THE FLYING BOAT

THE excitement of the bear fight and of being shut into the tunnel through the ice had for the moment driven out of the minds of all the party from the flying boat remembrance of the cause which had brought them here to the giant iceberg. For the time being even Tom had forgotten Mr. Damon and Mr. Nestor and their companions.

At least some of the castaways from the schooner *Kalrye* were right ahead of Tom's party. The booming voice of the excitable Wakefield Damon and his "blessing" could never be mistaken by anybody who knew him at all!

Captain Olaf Karofsen burst into a great roar of laughter, and, cheering loudly, he strode ahead along the passage.

"We bane findt dem fellers!" he bawled. "Misder Damon! How you vas now—yes?"

The others heard Mr. Damon cry:

"Here's that Skowegian, Nestor! Captain of the *Kalrye*. What do you know about this?

Bless my divining rod! I never expected to see him again."

The whole party, including Tom, followed the big captain. They rushed into a circular chamber in the ice. In the middle was a small fire burning on a piece of copper sheathing, set up on empty bean cans to keep the heat from the floor of the chamber.

There were only two persons present, both wrapped well in furs. They had been eating some cooked fish of some kind and drinking tea from tin pannikins. The man who had first got up to greet the newcomers was Mr. Wakefield Damon.

"Bless my horn spectacles!" he gasped, staring. "Is that Tom Swift I see? And Koku? And Ned Newton? Bless my imagination! I certainly must be seeing things."

"You surely are, Mr. Damon!" cried Ned. "You are seeing a bunch of castaways—just as much cast away as you are."

But Tom gave his closest attention to the other man—the man who still sat before the fire. There was no mistaking him, yet he looked so different from the wan and almost helpless man who had left Shopton for the Arctic weeks before that the young inventor could scarcely believe he was Mary Nestor's father.

"Mr. Nestor!" gasped Tom.

"Tom, my boy! Did you really come to find us? My brave fellow!"

"I did not come expecting to find such a picture of health, Mr. Nestor," declared Tom, clasping hands with the ex-invalid. "That crazy Raddiker wasn't so crazy as I feared, was he? Why, Mr. Nestor, you are a picture!"

"I am a picture of a homesick man, believe me," declared Mary's father earnestly. "I don't know how you got here, Tom; but I hope you can take us back home in a hurry."

"Bless my seven-leagued boots! how you must have traveled to get here so quickly, Tom Swift," Mr. Damon suddenly shouted. "How did you do it? I see the skipper must have got word of the wreck to you. But how did you fellows get here?"

"Through the air," said Ned, laughing.

"The new flying boat?" demanded Mr. Nestor. "Is it a success, Tom?"

"Bless my flying carpet of Bagdad!" chuckled Mr. Damon. "Never thought of that! Where is she? Can you take us all back?"

"We hope to. Though it may be close crowding with the five sailors. By the way," added Tom, "where are they?"

Instantly Mr. Wakefield Damon was very grave. Mr. Nestor said slowly:

"We had a terrible accident the third day we

were on this ice island. We were climbing over the heights, making for a place where we thought of setting up an oar with a flag, although it scarcely seemed possible that there would be any passing ship so late in the fall.

"However," he went on, "we came to a crevasse in the ice, and in trying to cross it two of the men fell and disappeared. We could not reach them."

"And bless my disappearing riches!" burst out Wakefield Damon, "the chest with my legacy from Aman Dele fell with them. We lost the men and the thirty thousand dollars in a moment."

"That is very unfortunate, Mr. Damon," said Tom seriously. "Where are the other three sailors who made up your party?"

"They are out somewhere now hunting for food—seals or fish, or the like. Brave fellows! Bless their hats and shoestrings! I mean that all of them shall be well paid for their faithfulness to us."

Captain Karofsen was silent. He had learned by a single question that the two sailors who had fallen into the chasm with the treasure chest were his own brother and his nephew! These relatives had aroused in the schooner captain a great desire to recover the castaways.

"Let's get out of here and find your other three helpers," Tom said finally. "We must get back to the gorge in which we left the flying boat. Brannigan will believe we are completely lost."

"And maybe we are," said Ned, again pessimistic. "No knowing whether we can get down into that valley again. And, once there, shall we be able to lift the *Winged Arrow* into the air?"

None of the others paid much attention to Ned's gloomy words. Mr. Damon and Mr. Nestor were too much interested in hearing news from home and Tom's brief account of the flight of the flying boat from America to Iceland and thence to this part of the Arctic Ocean to listen to Ned.

"It is wonderful!" declared Mr. Nestor. "One could scarcely believe that you would have so easily found this particular iceberg—and us upon it."

"Thanks to the bear," said Tom. "And if we get short of provisions we can go back and get a few bear steaks. Where is the entrance to this house?"

Mr. Nestor and Mr. Damon led the way. In two minutes they were out on the open ice, on the side of one of the ice hills over which the explorers had previously flown in the flying boat.

"How far are we from the place where we left the *Winged Arrow*, Captain?" asked Tom of Olaf Karofsen.

"It iss so far as that peak—yes? Maype ten mile. But my odder t'ree men——?"

Almost immediately the party sighted the trio of sailors coming up the slope from the ice field. Two of them bore a frozen seal between them. The other carried the guns and a rope. When they saw Captain Karofsen and the others they shrieked their joy and, dropping the seal, scrambled up the ice slope as fast as possible.

In their own language they broke into a concerted account of their adventures since the *Kalrye* had been wrecked. It was easy for the Americans to know when the sailors spoke of the loss of Captain Karofsen's brother and nephew. The schooner captain grew very, very grave.

"I wish we might search that chasm you speak of for those men," Tom whispered to Mr. Damon. "You say they carried a bag of provisions, too?"

"Bless my emergency ration, Tom Swift!" whispered the eccentric gentleman. "We yelled there and waited around for an hour. There was not a sound rose from that hole. They must have been instantly killed."

"But the money?"

"We-ell," said Mr. Damon doubtfully. "Of course, all I thought of at first was the chance of our getting away from here. But now it looks different. It might be well to make a search for the treasure box. But first, let us see," he added more vigorously, "if we can get your flying boat out of that hole you say she is in."

That actually was the main thing to worry
about.   And even when the party had reached
the brink of the gorge and fortunately found a
traversable path to the bottom of it and came in
sight of the flying boat, the question as to whether
or no they could get the *Winged Arrow* into the
air again was the all-important subject of their
thoughts.

CHAPTER XXIII

STILL CRIPPLED

BRANNIGAN and his associates had become extremely anxious because of the absence of the captain of the flying boat and his friends. And when they reappeared at the bottom of the gorge with five of the lost men of whom they had been in search, the mechanicians were inclined to think it almost a miraculous happening.

It was, however, rather a serious occasion. The fact that two of the castaways, as well as thirty thousand dollars in treasure, were utterly lost cast a cloud over all their minds.

Besides, although the mechanicians had repaired the airtight pontoon and rigged it to the end of the seaplane wing again, there was a question in all their minds as to whether the big flying boat could be raised from the bottom of the ice gorge without bringing her into collision again with the walls.

The five new passengers crowded the carrying quarters of the seaplane, too. She had not been

built with the idea of carrying more than twelve
people, and now there were sixteen. Tom believed that under a fair test the *Winged Arrow*
would sail with several tons more weight than
she had ever yet carried. But this jump-off was
going to be no fair test.

"We've got to take a chance," said the young
inventor.

"If only we are successful!" murmured Ned.

When they were all inside and the doors were
closed, the young inventor went over the machinery with great care, personally trying out
each part. He dared not empty the compressed
air tanks, although he would have liked to do
that until the plane had risen above the walls of
the gorge. The air was needed for balance, however; he was confident of that.

There was not room to turn the plane around
as she rested on her wheels and tail, the ice cliffs
were too near together; while ahead of her was
a very short straight run for her to gain the speed
to fly.

It was a ticklish undertaking. If, under the
thrust of her powerful motors, she went head on
into one wall or the other of the cañon, Tom was
pretty sure that the *Winged Arrow* would never
get out of the heart of this giant iceberg.

"If we leave both the plane and Mr. Damon's
treasure here in the ice, we shall certainly have

to mark this venture down as a total loss," murmured Tom, to his chum.

"Huh! we won't mark anything down," replied Ned. "We will have a hot time ever getting to land. Don't forget that."

"I am not likely to overlook it," confessed the young inventor. "I never had one of my inventions put to so severe a test before. And our lives, you must remember, depend upon the thing working right."

"Go on. Do your worst," urged Ned. "If I am to spend the rest of my natural life on this chunk of ice, I want to know it as soon as possible. Let's get it over."

Tom would not do a thing in haste, however. Not until he had made sure that the mechanism would work perfectly did he signal Brannigan to start his motors. He stood at the controls until the motors were roaring well before he started the propellers.

The huge boat began to move slowly. Almost at once she lifted under the pressure of the propellers. Her nose came up like the head of a spirited horse. Mr. Wakefield Damon gave voice to one of his excited explosions:

"Bless all my kites and balloons, she's going up!"

"That's what we want!" exclaimed Ned. "The higher, the better!"

She was going up! Better than she had ever taken the air before. Everybody in the pilot room broke into a cheer, and Tom Swift was as proud as ever he had felt before in his life over anything he had built.

Put to the severest sort of test, the *Winged Arrow* was making good. How proud his father would be when he told him of this jump-off from the bottom of the cleft in the huge iceberg! And Mary! Aside from the exploration party finding and rescuing her father, Tom knew that Mary Nestor would comprehend the feelings of the inventor of the flying boat which had made this success possible.

On a short slant skyward, the plane rose higher and higher. The long Arctic day was just ended, the sun had dropped below the horizon's edge, and a number of pale stars were showing in the vault above.

The flying boat scaled the heights of the ice cliffs and finally poised over the deep cleft in which they had spent so many uncertain hours. Tom believed that his task here was done. He meant to fly now to Iceland, as he had promised Captain Karofsen, and leave the schooner captain and his men at some handy port.

The young inventor had no intention of being entangled in any plot engendered by the Russian Government or its agents. Let all that be explained from America. He was sure that Monsieur Polansky had never obtained his credentials from the Navy Department by fair means and that there would be no real trouble awaiting him when he got back to Shopton.

He smiled upon Ned, who stood beside him, and began to wheel the flying boat till her nose pointed to the east. Somewhere in that direction—so far away that he could not see it—lay Iceland.

"What is that?" demanded Mr. Wakefield Damon suddenly. "Look at that smoke. Why, you'd think that ice mountain was a crater of a volcano! Bless my smokepipes! it is the equal of old Mount Hekla."

The phenomenon to which Mr. Damon pointed startled them all. A spiral of smoke seemed to be rising, as he said, out of the higher pinnacle of ice. The *Winged Arrow* was circling that peak. How was it possible for smoke to come out of a hole in the ice when, as far as they knew, there was no living human being on the berg they were leaving?

"Let's get around to the other side," cried Ned. "Goodness me! maybe there are other folks cast away here."

"It nefer is *dem?*" questioned Captain Olaf Karofsen excitedly.

Tom changed the controls. The great flying

boat heeled over a little as her nose drove into the wind. As she passed out from the shelter of the pinnacle of ice the power of the gale smote upon the seaplane as it had not before. The wind howled and whistled.

Tom signaled to the power room. for the compressed air pump to be started again. In this gale he realized the boat would roll, and this was dangerous. She needed more balance-weight.

Again, the structure rolled and groaned. Mr. Damon and Mr. Nestor cried. out. They had not experienced this motion before. The *Winged Arrow* came to an even keel, then once more dipped sideways.

With a crash one wing-end scraped along the hill of ice. The rebound carried the plane away from the wall of ice; but she began to descend, slowly but surely.

Tom speeded up, and the groaning boat shot away from the hillside. Behind them the spiral of smoke came from a cleft into which it had been impossible for any of them to see. The flying boat was flapping downward like a broken-winged bird!

"Are we wrecked? Is it a smash-up?" queried Mr. Nestor anxiously.

"Bless my anchors!" gasped Mr. Damon.

"We've got to make a landing," said Tom, with some show of cheerfulness. "But there is a pretty level field of ice to make it on.   I think we shall be all right."

The next moment the boat was bouncing on its wheels and tail.   The power had been shut off. Soon they came to a halt and it was possible to discover how badly the flying boat was damaged, if damaged at all.

CHAPTER XXIV

UNEXPECTED GOOD FORTUNE

MR. WAKEFIELD DAMON was possessed of a bulldog trait. When he once set his teeth into a thing he would not let go until he had mastered it.

While Tom and the others were giving way to excitement over the result to the flying boat of the shock it had undergone, Mr. Damon (when once the door in the hull was opened) leaped out and stared up the slope of the ice peak to see if he could again observe the curl of smoke which had been rising from that height as the flying boat passed over it.

"There is somebody up there. Bless my tortoise-shell glasses! there must be somebody up there. Smoke doesn't come out of a hill of ice by any natural means, that is sure."

But he did not see the smoke now. He called to Olaf Karofsen. He had picked up a few words of the Old Norse dialect much used by the people of the "back end" of Iceland, and the schooner captain spoke that language, too.

So the other Americans in the party did not understand what Mr. Damon and the captain were so excitedly talking about.

"What made that smoke, Captain?" demanded Mr. Damon.

"Fire," declared the man promptly.

"And fire in an iceberg is not a common thing. Over there is the crevasse where we lost your poor brother and his boy. Bless my icepick! but there is something strange about this."

"We will go see," declared the captain.

He hurried for a coil of rope and a rifle. Unnoticed by the others, the giant seaman and his employer climbed the slope of the ice mountain. Tom and his helpers were overhauling the airtight pontoon that swung from the left wing of the flying boat. This was the part injured by the latest collision.

"It must be that I am not so well able to judge distances as I was," the young inventor grumbled. "To smash a wing twice, hand running, as you might say!"

"It was a puff of wind did this for you," declared Ned. "I would not blame my eyesight."

To work in the open on the ice with a living gale blowing down from the Pole was by no means a comfortable situation. The mechanicians had to take turns in working on the broken wing and pontoon. A man might easily freeze his hands

while working without gloves. Two gasoline
stoves were brought out of the flying boat and
set up on the ice right where the repair gang
worked. The cook served hot coffee by the gal-
lon. The passengers did all they could to help,
but that was little.

Suddenly Mr. Nestor noticed the absence of
Mr. Damon and the schooner captain. He asked:

"Have they gone hunting? Why did they
climb that hill, do you suppose, Tom?"

"Didn't we see some smoke up there?" queried
Tom, only mildly interested. "Why, yes! Mr.
Damon was talking about smoke from the ice
peak, and that got me interested—interested
enough to scale the old plane across the shoulder
of that hill," and the young inventor laughed
rather ruefully.

"There's something going on up there, Mr.
Swift!" exclaimed Kingston suddenly. "See
there?"

He pointed up the heights. Several hundred
feet above the plain the big seaman was standing
and waving his arms wildly to attract attention.
Now his voice came booming down from the
eminence:

"Mis-der Swift! Mis-der Swift!" he sing-
songed. "Send up a couple of my bullies undt
a pread pag. Hurry oop!"

"Wonder what's going on up there," remarked

Ned, as Tom waved to a couple of the seamen to obey their skipper's demand.

"Let's have a look ourselves," Kingston said, and started up the ascent.

Tom could not go; but there was nothing to keep Ned back, so he fell in behind the wireless operator. Besides, one could keep warm on the ice only while in motion. The two young fellows swarmed up the hill as fast as they could travel, while the sailors came on in their rear with the bag.

Ned and his companion found Captain Karofsen on a little shelf of the hill. He was much excited and his face was again asmile.

"It iss wonderful! Wonderful!" he declared. "Come with me, young gentlemen. It is wonderful."

"I bet it is," commented Ned. "But just what is it?"

They fell in behind the excited captain of the *Kalrye,* who led them along the shelf, around an abrupt corner, and brought them out upon a small plateau in which there was a sink. Mr. Damon was lying flat upon his stomach and looking down into this chasm. He turned his red face toward Ned and Kingston and burst out with:

"Bless my Italian gardens! here is the most wonderful thing I ever saw. Did you bring that rope?"

"It's coming," said Ned. "What is the matter down there, Mr. Damon?"

"Greatest thing in the world, Ned!" exclaimed the eccentric gentleman. "The coincidence is wonderful. Who would ever have thought it! Well!"

"It's wonderful, all right," repeated the puzzled Ned. "Both you and Captain Karofsen say so. But just what *is* it?"

"Come here! See yonder? Half a mile or so away is the crevasse down which those two unfortunate men tumbled who were carrying my chest of Danish gold. We never expected to see them again—or the chest. And I guess the chest *is* done for," admitted the excited Mr. Damon.

Ned and the operator were now beside him. They knelt on the ice and likewise peered down into the blue-white depths of the sink. Ned uttered a shout of amazement.

"What do you know about this!" murmured Kingston.

Under an out-thrust shelf of ice and on the bottom of the hole a small fire was smouldering. Two muffled figures lay beside this tiny fire. But they moved, first one and then the other raising his head and then waving a feeble hand to the spectators on the brink of the ice wall.

"The lost seamen?" demanded New Newton of Mr. Damon.

"Karofsen's brother and nephew," the gentleman answered. "I don't care about the lost gold! The men are still alive! They must have suffered terribly. And how they found fuel for even that little fire, I don't see."

The eager schooner captain just then arrived with the pair of seamen he had called. They had a coil of rope long enough to reach to the bottom of the cleft in the ice.

It was plain that the men below could not help themselves. Kingston, who was the lightest of the party, volunteered to go down.

"Take the pag vonce," said Karofsen eagerly. "I pet you it vill come handy—yes? Now, are you ready?"

The operator swung out from the ice, and fending himself from the wall with feet and hands, was lowered safely to the floor of the sink. As soon as he stood upon his feet there he disengaged himself from the loop of the rope and ran across to the two men.

They tried to struggle up, but both dropped back. They were weak from lack of nourishment and their extremities were undoubtedly frost-bitten. The older man insisted by gestures (he could speak but few English words) that Kingston aid his son, first of all.

The wireless operator seized the boy in his arms and staggered across the sink with him.

He fastened him safely in the noose and gave the signal for those above to "hoist away."

Although the turning body of the youth scraped several times against the ice, he was not hurt while his uncle and the sailors drew him up. Kingston, when he saw him swinging near the top, ran back to the other man. The latter had struggled to his knees and seized the bread bag that Kingston had brought down with him by Karofsen's advice.

What he wished to do with the bag puzzled Kingston for a moment. Then he saw what had been cached under the overshot ledge of ice, well back against the wall.

"Right-o, my man!" the operator cried. "I am wise to it. Here! Let me do all that. We'll send the bag up before you go up. I quite understand."

He was much excited. And the situation was indeed an exciting one. Kingston knew that the spectators at the top of the ice cliff were going to feel much amazement when that bread bag swung up there at the end of the noose.

The heavy bag swung out of his sight. Then came a yell. Mr. Damon almost fell over the brink of the wall.

"Bless my coupon bonds and the interest on my mortgages, these courageous men have saved my thirty thousand dollars! It's gold! They broke up the chest to make a fire, but here is the money intact.

"Here, Olaf! Swing your brother up here in a hurry. I want to hug him. Bless my last red cent! if we get off of this giant iceberg alive, he and his boy shall never know want as long as they live.

"Lay onto the line, lads! Now, haul! Bless my hemp and cordage! If that line parts now, we'll lose one of the most honest men who ever walked on two feet. Altogether, now!"

CHAPTER XXV

BACK FROM THE ARCTIC

THE line did not break. The captain's brother was drawn to the top of the low cliff. After that Kingston was raised. The delighted Wakefield Damon was talking all the time and could scarcely wait to help bear the two exhausted seamen down the hill to where the flying boat was being repaired.

Captain Karofsen carried the bag of gold coin over his shoulder, while the other five from the flying boat bore the exhausted sailors down the slope. When Tom and the others saw them coming they were likewise excited. The recovery of these two men completed the rescue of the party of castaways to search for whom the *Winged Arrow* had been brought by her inventor from the States.

"Nothing to be put down on the debit side of the column, Tom!" shouted Ned, when he drew near. "If you can make the old plane ride again, we can figure that we've turned the trick."

"And Mr. Damon's fortune?" shouted Tom.

"Bless my Russian rubles!" chortled Mr. Damon, "I could buy up the entire Russian Government monetary output now. Here is Aman Dele's treasure that he willed me. I am a lucky man. And these brave fellows shall share in my good luck."

He was as good as his word. It may as well be said here that Mr. Damon, with all his eccentricities, was a very honorable man. He reimbursed Captain Karofsen for his time and exertions, gave each of the sailors a handsome present, and to the captain's brother and son he made over a trust fund that, as he had declared, would keep the two injured men from want for the remainder of their lives.

For the two who had fallen down the crevasse with the treasure chest had been exposed so long to the frost that it would be months before they would be able to go to sea. All these good offices, however, Mr. Damon arranged later through a legal representative.

Just now the entire party was anxious to discover if the *Winged Arrow* would fly. Half the short Arctic night had been expended in these recent exertions. Brannigan and his men had taken the tools and the gasoline stoves back into the ship. They all climbed aboard as soon as possible and once more preparations were made for a jump-off.

"If this old plane doesn't act right now," said Tom, "I'll take her home and break her up for scrap. That's a promise."

"If you get her home at all," said Ned. "I hope she won't get temperamental about the time we are over the Newfoundland fishing banks, for instance."

Their first destination, of course, was Iceland. The flying boat was overcrowded, and Tom wished to place Captain Karofsen and his five men somewhere near their own homes before launching out for the longer flight for America across the North Atlantic.

Tom's first anxiety, however, was to get the huge flying boat into the air and learn if she would respond properly to the controls. The motors raced all right when they were tried, and he believed that he knew now just how much compressed air to order pumped into the skin of the hull.

Yet he signaled Brannigan and stood at the controls when the time came for the jump-off with a feeling of anxiety. How would the boat act? If the whole party were marooned on this iceberg as Mr. Damon and Mr. Nestor and the five sailors had been, who would come to their rescue?

"Not a chance!" Ned answered to these queries.

"All ready, Bran?" called Tom into the tube.

"Aye, aye, boss!" exclaimed the mechanician.

The hull of the flying boat began to tremble. The ice field ahead of her was quite clear of rubble and there were no chasms. The propeller began to spin and the boat rolled forward.

Trembling, shaking like some huge fowl trying to take the air, the *Winged Arrow* started. She cocked her nose skyward and left the ice. Up, up she soared, on a long slant into the east. The motors throbbed rhythmically while the gale whistled through the stays.

Tom felt the pull of the controls and knew that the slight rocking of the boat betrayed a good balance. On a graceful curve she left the surface of the iceberg and leaped out over the tumbling, open sea.

There was a wide channel between this huge berg and the nearest field of ice. Flocks of Arctic sea birds rose whirring beneath the flying boat. On the edge of the ice they saw two solemn looking polar bears fishing for seals. Sea lions played on one shelving beach of ice.

"Farewell to the giant iceberg!" shouted Ned, as the *Winged Arrow* left the mountain of crystal behind. "I hope I don't see any ice again for a year—not even next summer! B-r-r-r! Shall we ever be really warm again?"

They were packed so close in the cabin and

pilot room of the flying boat that they should have been more than ordinarily warm. It was indeed an uncomfortable journey to the nearest land.

Captain Karofsen had studied the chart and he marked a little town near Reykjavik where Tom could make a landing without attracting attention from the authorities of the island. Of course it would have been a simple matter to get by cablegram from the United States information that would show the Governor of Iceland that the Russians were trying to steal the flying boat. But that might delay the party for several weeks.

And nobody was more eager than Tom to get back to Shopton. He confided to Captain Karofsen certain messages to be sent to Mr. Barton Swift and Mary Nestor, for he expected that the flying boat would be all of three days on the journey home, even if she did not have to descend for repairs.

He made the landing on the spot Captain Karofsen pointed out, with success. Nothing needed adjusting, and five minutes after taking the ground the seamen and their captain were out of the flying boat. Then, after getting a supply of gasoline and oil, the latter made another jump-off.

"The old plane is doing you proud, Tom!"

cried Ned, when they were in the air again. "Just keep away from icebergs, and I feel sure you will have no trouble with her. But believe me! if you take another flight into the Arctic, you can count me out."

In several ways the wonderful voyage of the *Winged Arrow* had never been equaled by any flying boat. Her long jump over the Atlantic proved her to be a unique craft. She could remain in the air at her pilot's will. She had proved that she could rest in rough water. And the usage she had received on the giant iceberg showed her to be a craft able to endure a deal of knocking about.

Naturally, when she returned to Shopton, she was not the spick and span looking flying boat that she had been when she left that base for the Arctic. Nevertheless, her inventor was satisfied that he knew now just what he could do with her.

"Will you sell her to the Navy Department if they want her, Tom?" asked Mr. Nestor, during the flight home.

"I am going to sell her to nobody. Not even to the Russian Government," said Tom, smiling. "We are in no war now, thank goodness, and I mean to keep and improve this craft until she can be no further perfected. Of course," he added loyally, "she will be at the service of the country at any time she may be needed."

"There is a whole lot I can do to her yet to make her of more value both in war and commerce. I wish I might make these improvements, however, without so much publicity. The Swift Construction Company is getting into the papers too much." Then he grinned suddenly. "You know, after all, what I want is a quiet life."

Ned, listening to this, made an awful face.

"Whoo!" he shouted. "The sort of quiet life Tom Swift wants would make a jumping jack hysterical! Tom, you know you could not keep quiet and give up adventures if you had five hundred times the fortune Mr. Damon is bringing home with him from Iceland."

"Bless my foreign exchange!" exclaimed Mr. Damon, "that is a true word you said, Ned Newton. Why, anybody who has anything to do with Tom Swift is bound to get into the most exciting situations——"

"Listen to him!" cried Tom.

"We know who is the person who manages to get into trouble without any help," declared Mr. Nestor laughing. "I certainly am obliged to Brother Damon for taking me to the Arctic. It has restored my health. I feel like another man again.

"Nevertheless, if Wakefield Damon asks me to walk down street with him to buy a necktie after this, I shall be afraid to accompany him. Something unexpected is bound to happen when one is in that gentleman's company."

"Bless my reputation!" groaned the eccentric gentleman, "have you all such an opinion of me as this? I declare! I will go home and raise fancy chickens and nothing shall entice me on another journey. Humph! That is, until Tom Swift decides to start off to the antipodes. I could not contain myself at home if I knew he was away junketing."

Forewarned of the coming of the flying boat, half the population of Shopton and all Tom's workmen were awaiting its appearance. Tom brought the *Winged Arrow* over the field behind the shops, spiraled down, and took the ground very lightly. When they opened the door in the side of the hull the first faces they saw were those of Mary Nestor and her mother and Mr. Barton Swift and his faithful attendant, Eradicate Sampson.

When Rad set his eyes on the gigantic Koku he cried out:

"Ma goodness, Mars' Tom! couldn't you lose dat big nuisance up da in de Antic Seas somewhar? He suah ain't much good 'round yere.

I reckoned he'd make good polar bear bait, or de like. Has I got to feed him again?"

Koku showed his teeth in a wide smile. "No polum bear kill Koku," he declared, leaping out of the flying boat and beginning to strut. "Koku kill bear. Killum with spear. Koku great chief."

"Koku great nuisance," grumbled Rad, grabbing the big fellow by the arm. "Come on wid me. I got a beefsteak ha'f as big as a bedsheet to brile for yo'. Yo' suah isn't much good, but we got to feed yo'."

Mr. Nestor was welcomed by his wife and daughter almost as though he had risen from the grave. His improvement in health was so great that they could not cease exclaiming over it.

Tom and his other friends from the flying boat were all greeted most hilariously by the crowd. The mechanicians and Kingston had their stories to tell. Ned hurried away on business. Mr. Barton Swift wrung his son's hand.

"I was afraid for a while that that strange Russian would manage to make you trouble. Admiral Gilder found out about him soon after you had started on your cruise. The fellow had got credentials from the Navy Board by trickery."

"If the Soviet Government had had a bunch of flying men up there at Reykjavik, ready to hop aboard the craft when they got us out and under guard," said Tom, "they might have managed to get the *Winged Arrow* as far as Russia, and we would have whistled for any money. Their printing presses could not print rubles fast enough to pay me for this flying boat."

"Then you consider her a success, Tom?" asked Mr. Swift smiling.

"She most certainly is. As far as I have gone I am satisfied. But I have not finished with her yet. You wait and see, Dad."

Then he hurried away to join Mary Nestor. And, after what Tom had done for the young girl's father, the reader may believe that what Mary Nestor said to Tom made him blush to the tips of his ears!

THE END

THE TOM SWIFT SERIES
By VICTOR APPLETON

UNIFORM STYLE OF BINDING.   INDIVIDUAL COLORED WRAPPERS.

These spirited tales, convey in a realistic way, the wonderful advances in land and sea locomotion. Stories like these are impressed upon the memory and their reading is productive only of good.

TOM SWIFT AND HIS MOTOR CYCLE
TOM SWIFT AND HIS MOTOR BOAT
TOM SWIFT AND HIS AIRSHIP
TOM SWIFT AND HIS SUBMARINE BOAT
TOM SWIFT AND HIS ELECTRIC RUNABOUT
TOM SWIFT AND HIS WIRELESS MESSAGE
TOM SWIFT AMONG THE DIAMOND MAKERS
TOM SWIFT IN THE CAVES OF ICE
TOM SWIFT AND HIS SKY RACER
TOM SWIFT AND HIS ELECTRIC RIFLE
TOM SWIFT IN THE CITY OF GOLD
TOM SWIFT AND HIS AIR GLIDER
TOM SWIFT IN CAPTIVITY
TOM SWIFT AND HIS WIZARD CAMERA
TOM SWIFT AND HIS GREAT SEARCHLIGHT
TOM SWIFT AND HIS GIANT CANNON
TOM SWIFT AND HIS PHOTO TELEPHONE
TOM SWIFT AND HIS AERIAL WARSHIP
TOM SWIFT AND HIS BIG TUNNEL
TOM SWIFT IN THE LAND OF WONDERS
TOM SWIFT AND HIS WAR TANK
TOM SWIFT AND HIS AIR SCOUT
TOM SWIFT AND HIS UNDERSEA SEARCH
TOM SWIFT AMONG THE FIRE FIGHTERS
TOM SWIFT AND HIS ELECTRIC LOCOMOTIVE

GROSSET & DUNLAP,   PUBLISHERS,   NEW YORK

THE MOVING PICTURE BOYS SERIES

BY VICTOR APPLETON

UNIFORM STYLE OF BINDING.   INDIVIDUAL COLORED WRAPPERS.

Moving pictures and photo plays are famous the world over, and in this line of books the reader is given a full description of how the films are made—the scenes of little dramas, indoors and out, trick pictures to satisfy the curious, soul-stirring pictures of city affairs, life in the Wild West, among the cowboys and Indians, thrilling rescues along the seacoast, the daring of picture hunters in the jungle among savage beasts, and the great risks run in picturing conditions in a land of earthquakes. The volumes teem with adventures and will be found interesting from first chapter to last.

THE MOVING PICTURE BOYS

THE MOVING PICTURE BOYS IN THE WEST

THE MOVING PICTURE BOYS ON THE COAST

THE MOVING PICTURE BOYS IN THE JUNGLE

THE MOVING PICTURE BOYS IN EARTH-
                              QUAKE LAND

THE MOVING PICTURE BOYS AND THE FLOOD

THE MOVING PICTURE BOYS AT PANAMA

THE MOVING PICTURE BOYS UNDER THE SEA

THE MOVING PICTURE BOYS ON THE WAR
                              FRONT

THE MOVING PICTURE BOYS ON FRENCH
                              BATTLEFIELDS

MOVING PICTURE BOYS' FIRST SHOWHOUSE

MOVING PICTURE BOYS AT SEASIDE PARK

MOVING PICTURE BOYS ON BROADWAY

THE MOVING PICTURE BOYS' OUTDOOR
                              EXHIBITION

THE MOVING PICTURE BOYS' NEW IDEA

GROSSET & DUNLAP,   PUBLISHERS,   NEW YORK

THE BOBBSEY TWINS BOOKS

For Little Men and Women
By LAURA LEE HOPE
Author of "The Bunny Brown" Series, Etc.

12mo. DURABLY BOUND. ILLUSTRATED. UNIFORM STYLE OF BINDING

Copyright publications which cannot be obtained elsewhere. Books that charm the hearts of the little ones, and of which they never tire.

THE BOBBSEY TWINS

THE BOBBSEY TWINS IN THE COUNTRY

THE BOBBSEY TWINS AT THE SEASHORE

THE BOBBSEY TWINS AT SCHOOL

THE BOBBSEY TWINS AT SNOW LODGE

THE BOBBSEY TWINS ON A HOUSEBOAT

THE BOBBSEY TWINS AT MEADOW BROOK

THE BOBBSEY TWINS AT HOME

THE BOBBSEY TWINS IN A GREAT CITY

THE BOBBSEY TWINS ON BLUEBERRY ISLAND

THE BOBBSEY TWINS ON THE DEEP BLUE SEA

THE BOBBSEY TWINS IN THE GREAT WEST

Grosset & Dunlap, Publishers, New York

THE BUNNY BROWN SERIES
By LAURA LEE HOPE
Author of the Popular "Bobbsey Twins" Books

Wrapper and text illustrations drawn by
FLORENCE ENGLAND NOSWORTHY

12mo. DURABLY BOUND. ILLUSTRATED. UNIFORM STYLE OF BINDING

These stories by the author of the "Bobbsey Twins" Books are eagerly welcomed by the little folks from about five to ten years of age. Their eyes fairly dance with delight at the lively doings of inquisitive little Bunny Brown and his cunning, trustful sister Sue.

Bunny was a lively little boy, very inquisitive. When he did anything, Sue followed his leadership. They had many adventures, some comical in the extreme.

BUNNY BROWN AND HIS SISTER SUE

BUNNY BROWN AND HIS SISTER SUE ON GRAND-PA'S FARM

BUNNY BROWN AND HIS SISTER SUE PLAYING CIRCUS

BUNNY BROWN AND HIS SISTER SUE AT CAMP REST-A-WHILE

BUNNY BROWN AND HIS SISTER SUE AT AUNT LU'S CITY HOME

BUNNY BROWN AND HIS SISTER SUE IN THE BIG WOODS

BUNNY BROWN AND HIS SISTER SUE ON AN AUTO TOUR

BUNNY BROWN AND HIS SISTER SUE AND THEIR SHETLAND PONY

BUNNY BROWN AND HIS SISTER SUE GIVING A SHOW

BUNNY BROWN AND HIS SISTER SUE AT CHRIST-MAS TREE COVE

GROSSET & DUNLAP, PUBLISHERS, NEW YORK

THE OUTDOOR CHUMS SERIES

By CAPTAIN QUINCY ALLEN.

The outdoor chums are four wide-awake lads, sons of wealthy men of a small city located on a lake. The boys love outdoor life, and are greatly interested in hunting, fishing, and picture taking. They have motor cycles, motor boats, canoes, etc., and during their vacations go everywhere and have all sorts of thrilling adventures. The stories give full directions for camping out, how to fish, how to hunt wild animals and prepare the skins for stuffing, how to manage a canoe, how to swim, etc. Full of the spirit of outdoor life.

THE OUTDOOR CHUMS
Or The First Tour of the Rod, Gun and Camera Club.

THE OUTDOOR CHUMS ON THE LAKE
Or Lively Adventures on Wildcat Island.

THE OUTDOOR CHUMS IN THE FOREST
Or Laying the Ghost of Oak Ridge.

THE OUTDOOR CHUMS ON THE GULF
Or Rescuing the Lost Balloonists.

THE OUTDOOR CHUMS AFTER BIG GAME
Or Perilous Adventures in the Wilderness.

THE OUTDOOR CHUMS ON A HOUSEBOAT
Or The Rivals of the Mississippi.

THE OUTDOOR CHUMS IN THE BIG WOODS
Or The Rival Hunters at Lumber Run.

THE OUTDOOR CHUMS AT CABIN POINT
Or The Golden Cup Mystery.

12mo. Averaging 240 pages. Illustrated. Handsomely bound in Cloth.

GROSSET & DUNLAP,   PUBLISHERS,   NEW YORK

THE GIRLS OF CENTRAL HIGH SERIES

By GERTRUDE W. MORRISON

12mo. BOUND IN CLOTH.   ILLUSTRATED.   UNIFORM STYLE OF BINDING.

Here is a series full of the spirit of high school life of to-day. The girls are real flesh-and-blood characters, and we follow them with interest in school and out. There are many contested matches on track and field, and on the water, as well as doings in the classroom and on the school stage. There is plenty of fun and excitement, all clean, pure and wholesome.

THE GIRLS OF CENTRAL HIGH
Or Rivals for all Honors.
> A stirring tale of high school life, full of fun, with a touch of mystery and a strange initiation.

THE GIRLS OF CENTRAL HIGH ON LAKE LUNA
Or The Crew That Won.
> Telling of water sports and fun galore, and of fine times in camp.

THE GIRLS OF CENTRAL HIGH AT BASKETBALL
Or The Great Gymnasium Mystery.
> Here we have a number of thrilling contests at basketball and in addition, the solving of a mystery which had bothered the high school authorities for a long while.

THE GIRLS OF CENTRAL HIGH ON THE STAGE
Or The Play That Took the Prize.
> How the girls went in for theatricals and how one of them wrote a play which afterward was made over for the professional stage and brought in some much-needed money.

THE GIRLS OF CENTRAL HIGH ON TRACK AND FIELD
Or The Girl Champions of the School League
> This story takes in high school athletics in their most approved and up-to-date fashion. Full of fun and excitement.

THE GIRLS OF CENTRAL HIGH IN CAMP
Or The Old Professor's Secret.
> The girls went camping on Acorn Island and had a delightful time at boating, swimming and picnic parties.

GROSSET & DUNLAP,   PUBLISHERS,   NEW YORK

THE MOVING PICTURE GIRLS SERIES

By LAURA LEE HOPE

Author of "The Bobbsey Twins Series."

12mo. BOUND IN CLOTH.   ILLUSTRATED.   UNIFORM STYLE OF BINDING

The adventures of Ruth and Alice DeVere. Their father, a widower, is an actor who has taken up work for the "movies." Both girls wish to aid him in his work and visit various localities to act in all sorts of pictures.

THE MOVING PICTURE GIRLS
Or First Appearance in Photo Dramas.

Having lost his voice, the father of the girls goes into the movies and the girls follow. Tells how many "parlor dramas" are filmed.

THE MOVING PICTURE GIRLS AT OAK FARM
Or Queer Happenings While Taking Rural Plays.

Full of fun in the country, the haps and mishaps of taking film plays, and giving an account of two unusual discoveries.

THE MOVING PICTURE GIRLS SNOWBOUND
Or The Proof on the Film.

A tale of winter adventures in the wilderness, showing how the photo-play actors sometimes suffer.

THE MOVING PICTURE GIRLS UNDER THE PALMS
Or Lost in the Wilds of Florida.

How they went to the land of palms, played many parts in dramas before the camera; were lost, and aided others who were also lost.

THE MOVING PICTURE GIRLS AT ROCKY RANCH
Or Great Days Among the Cowboys.

All who have ever seen moving pictures of the great West will want to know just how they are made. This volume gives every detail and is full of clean fun and excitement.

THE MOVING PICTURE GIRLS AT SEA
Or a Pictured Shipwreck that Became Real.

A thrilling account of the girls' experiences on the water.

THE MOVING PICTURE GIRLS IN WAR PLAYS
Or The Sham Battles at Oak Farm.

The girls play important parts in big battle scenes and have plenty of hard work along with considerable fun.

GROSSET & DUNLAP,   PUBLISHERS,   NEW YORK

THE OUTDOOR GIRLS SERIES
By LAURA LEE HOPE
Author of the popular "Bobbsey Twin Books" and "Bunny Brown" Series.

UNIFORM STYLE OF BINDING. INDIVIDUAL COLORED WRAPPERS.

These tales take in the various adventures participated in by several bright, up-to-date girls who love outdoor life. They are clean and wholesome, free from sensationalism, and absorbing from the first chapter to the last.

THE OUTDOOR GIRLS OF DEEPDALE
Or Camping and Tramping for Fun and Health.

THE OUTDOOR GIRLS AT RAINBOW LAKE
Or Stirring Cruise of the Motor Boat Gem.

THE OUTDOOR GIRLS IN A MOTOR CAR
Or The Haunted Mansion of Shadow Valley.

THE OUTDOOR GIRLS IN A WINTER CAMP
Or Glorious Days on Skates and Ice Boats.

THE OUTDOOR GIRLS IN FLORIDA
Or Wintering in the Sunny South.

THE OUTDOOR GIRLS AT OCEAN VIEW
Or The Box that Was Found in the Sand.

THE OUTDOOR GIRLS ON PINE ISLAND
Or A Cave and What it Contained.

THE OUTDOOR GIRLS IN ARMY SERVICE
Or Doing Their Bit for Uncle Sam.

THE OUTDOOR GIRLS AT THE HOSTESS HOUSE
Or Doing Their Best for the Soldiers.

THE OUTDOOR GIRLS AT BLUFF POINT
Or A Wreck and A Rescue.

THE OUTDOOR GIRLS AT WILD ROSE LODGE
Or The Hermit of Moonlight Falls.

THE OUTDOOR GIRLS IN THE SADDLE
Or The Girl Miner of Gold Run.

GROSSET & DUNLAP,   PUBLISHERS,   NEW YORK